# ADRIFT

# DRIFT

PAUL GRIFFIN

SCHOLASTIC INC.

Library of Congress Cataloging-in-Publication Data available

ISBN 978-0-545-87195-2

10 9 8 7 6 5 4 3 2 1 15 16 17 18 19

Printed in the U.S.A. 40
First printing 2015

Book design by Yaffa Jaskoll and Carol Ly

For Anna Orchard

# 1

**SAILOR'S ALMANAC, *LONG-RANGE FORECAST, NORTH ATLANTIC CORRIDOR: Summer will be lovely with mild winds through August, heading into hurricane season.***

The surfers called it The End for its killer waves. To everyone else it was the end of Long Island. Montauk. It's a town of beaches and bluffs on the tip of the south fork. My best friend, John Costello, and I landed summer jobs at a state park out there. My parents owned a flower shop, and one of their customers was a big deal in the parks department. I'd just finished junior year. The plan was to apply early decision to Yale as a forestry major. I dreamed of being a ranger in the Utah canyons or Alaska glaciers. I had to get out of the city. Everywhere I looked I saw Mr. Costello's ghost.

The name of the park was Heron Hills. I fixed boardwalks and lifeguard chairs and the dock struts rotting away in the saltwater marsh. When the tide was out, the seaweed crackled beneath a sun hot enough to melt your mind. My head ached no matter how much Gatorade I drank. I loved it, being deep in the quiet, near the water. From the bluffs I saw the earth's curve.

After work on the hottest day in August I met up with John in the park's vehicle maintenance shop. He'd been working in gas stations since the day after his dad's funeral, when he grabbed a job filling tires. Iceman. That's what everybody called him. We hadn't been able to hang out as much since we started going to different schools freshman year. I took the test for Hudson, a selective public school in Manhattan. It was a forty-minute train ride and a world away from Woodhull, a working-class neighborhood that straddles the Brooklyn–Queens border. John and I grew up there, right on the borderline. The high school in Woodhull was pretty rough, but John didn't care. All he needed was a diploma for trade school. He had his heart set on being an electrician, like his dad. Not his heart, his mind. Electrical work was sensible, steady.

The vehicle maintenance shop was stifling. John hoisted an engine out of a Land Rover with two other guys. They were sweating so much they looked like they'd gone swimming. John worked just as hard, but he was dry until one of the trucks backfired. I flinched too.

We hit the beach and swam out past where the waves broke and the water turned silky. We came in clear-eyed and hungry and stopped to say hi to a man who fished from knee-deep water. He gave us a pair of blues. I smothered them with butter and hand-mashed lemon and pan-cooked them in the fire pit behind the trailer where we bunked.

After dinner the harmonicas came out. Mr. Costello had taught us how to play, and John was good. The stars curved out of the dusk into the night. We never said much. We were good at being alone together. But that night it was on my mind. "You don't talk about it ever," I said. "About him."

John tended the fire with a broken slat he'd pulled from the dune fence. "Not until you make me anyway," he said. He checked his beat-up Timex and headed for the trailer. "The bugs are getting bad. Don't fall asleep out here again."

I buried the fire with sand. The waves caught the moonlight. One rose higher than the others, rolled toward me, and faded into the shore. The mosquitoes chased me into the trailer. I cracked my laptop to study for a little while before bed. I was taking a certified first responder course with the lifeguards. I wanted to know how to bring somebody back to life. I was learning what I already knew: Most times you can't. Anyway, it would look good on my Yale application.

# 2

We were at the mini-mart when it opened. Sundays we made extra money selling soda and ice cream. We packed the coolers with Klondike bars. The mini-mart was one of the few places you could raise a Wi-Fi signal. I texted all's well to my folks and downloaded a library book. The old man behind the counter scrambled us some eggs. "What are we reading this week, my friend? Another travelogue?"

"I keep telling him, he can run but he can't hide," John said.

"He'll do as he pleases," the old man said. "I suspect your friend's a genius."

"Not even close," I said.

"Own your greatness, son. False humility doesn't become a gentleman."

It wasn't false. Yes, I got good grades, but only because I studied as if my life depended on getting into Yale. I was average with an above-average ambition to break out of my neighborhood.

Blankets and bikinis covered the sand. Kids and gulls screamed. We lugged the coolers up and down the beach. "Ice cream here. Get your ice cream here." The heat in the sand went through my flip-flops. By noon I had five hundred dollars in my pocket. Yale money, if I got in. My grades and scores put me at the borderline. Always the borderline.

We restocked the coolers, but by the time we got back to the beach another hawker team was working our territory. We were taller, they were wider. They wore trendy shades and went shirtless and slick with Hawaiian Tropic. John and I wore T-shirts, hats, and sunscreen. We were dark anyway, the typical Woodhull mix, Irish and Italian. We both had black hair, but my mom is northern Italian, and my eyes are blue. John's dad was from the south, Sicilian, and John's eyes were black. He squinted at the muscle-heads, then at me. "Breathe," he said.

"You're officially done for the day," the bigger one said. "Dude, you deaf?"

John edged me back. "We'll make more money at Sully's anyway," he said.

I turned east toward Sully's Inn and the private beach where we could hawk our sugar for twice as much.

"Slow it down," John said. "Matt?"

"What?"

"Like we're walking underwater, right? Nice and easy."

"You see me running?" I said.

"Inside you are," John said.

The coolers weighed sixty pounds each. We stopped to catch our breath. A beat-up gull swooped in and pecked at a cigarette filter. Broken mussel shells spiked the beach. A mile later the sand smoothed out, combed clean and white. Painted hand fans waved like the wings of heat-doped butterflies. We couldn't be calling out like vendors working the cheap seats. We walked along the rows of chaise lounges and waited to be summoned. Back at the public beach the bathing suits were hot pink and yellow. At Sully's the bikinis were black. The women wore wide-brim white hats, except for this one girl down by the water.

Her dreadlocks dropped to her waist. She dressed them with light blue beads. She was tall, curvy, dark. Her smile was crooked in the most perfect way. Her eyes were the color of the ocean that day, the lightest green. She was so pretty I stopped walking. I wiped the sweat from my eyes and pretended the heat was making me dizzy.

She was helping this little kid build a simple sand castle, fast, between when the waves rolled up the shore. It was a turret really, a flipped sand bucket and then a flipped Dixie cup on top of that.

The wind blew their laughter my way. "Hurry," the girl said. She helped the kid put a shell on top of the castle just before the wave destroyed it. She and the little boy screamed. "It's just completely *gone*," the kid said.

The girl smoothed his hair. "That's why you have to remember it. Then it lives forever."

My phone buzzed. *I'm by the pool. Out of Coke.*

I found John and restocked him, and we split up to cover the beach. I looked back to the shoreline for the girl, but she was gone.

"I'm over here," she called out. She was sitting with a girl and a guy. The other girl was pretty too but thinner and blond. The guy was blond too, a giant with a giant smile. I figured they were my age, maybe a little older.

The skinny girl waved me over. "Let's see what you got there," she said. She had an accent, French maybe.

I lifted the cooler top. "Cokes are five bucks and Klondikes are—"

"Whatever you are charging is fine," the guy said. "Three of each, please." He had the same accent. He held out a credit card.

The girl with the blue-beaded hair said, "What's he supposed to do with that, slide it through his butt crack?" Her accent was prep school, Upper East Side.

"Either of you have any cash then?" the guy said. "Of course not." He winked at me. "They think I should pay for everything."

"That's what you're here for," the skinny girl said.

The one with the blue beads eyed me like she was studying the model at the Cro-Magnon exhibit. *There's something here I recognize as vaguely human, but . . .*

"Don't worry about it," I said. "You can catch me next time." That was it. Giving away three slightly melted Klondike bars. That's what started the wild ride that remapped the course of my life.

"That is amazingly sweet of you," the girl with beaded hair said.

The skinny girl asked, "You don't have any Diet?"

"This nice boy gives you a soda, and you trample his gift?" the nice girl said.

"*Tram*ple?" Skinny said.

The giant laughed, not in a nasty way. He had a good laugh, real.

John had Diet in his cooler. I waved him over, plucked a can from the soupy ice, and handed it to the skinny girl.

The more beautiful girl thanked me and said, "Driana. That one over there is my extremely obnoxious cousin Estefania. Her long-suffering boyfriend is João."

"JoJo," he said, shaking our hands.

"Matt and John," I said.

"That's cute," Estefania said. "Like Mutt and Jeff. This is how you say it, yes?"

"Where you guys from?" I said.

"*Você não falam Português?*" Estefania said.

"Portugal?" I said.

Estefania rolled her eyes, JoJo chuckled. "Rio," he said.

"That's in Brazil," Estefania said to let us know she thought we were uncultured morons, and we were. The farthest south I'd been was Staten Island.

"*I'm* from New York," Driana said, as if she wouldn't be caught dead coming from Rio.

"Us too," I said.

"I know," she said. Her lips curled into that killer smile.

I looked at John. He checked his Timex.

"John doesn't say much," Estefania said.

"Stef, run on up to the pool and dive to the bottom," Driana said. "We'll meet you there in twenty minutes."

"Come surfing with us," JoJo said.

Neither of us had ever touched a surfboard. "We have to sell this stuff before it melts," John said.

"When you're done," JoJo said. "Please, I want to thank you for the ice creams."

"He doesn't want to trample your gift," Stef said.

"We go out later," JoJo said, ignoring Stef. "When the beach empties and there aren't any little kids in the water."

"They don't know how to surf. Right, John?" Stef extended her long, tanned leg to kick a little sand at John.

JoJo didn't seem to mind that his girlfriend was flirting with another guy. "I'll teach you," he said. "It's a flying dream, except it tastes salty. You don't have to be afraid of us. We're the nice kind of rich people."

"No, we're not," Stef said.

"Nicer than the rest of the people here," JoJo said.

Stef put her hand to her mouth to whisper to John, except she shouted so everybody at Sully's would have to hear her. "They don't like us because Dri is brown." She pronounced her cousin's name like *dream* without the *m*. "Thank God we have more money than they do."

JoJo laughed; Driana rolled her eyes. Stef's assessment might have been right though. Take away the tans, that beach in front of Sully's was Mayflower, top deck.

"Meet us in an hour," JoJo said.

"They won't come." Stef pouted. "Dri, make John come. I'll be devastated if he doesn't." She looked genuinely sad.

John frowned. "Matt, let's go."

"Thanks anyway," I said.

A kid a few chairs down called to us. He couldn't have been ten. "Over here," he commanded. I felt like a dog that had been caught stealing table food. The kid wanted me to keep the change though.

Driana jogged up and pressed something into my hand. "Tuesday night," she said. "Party at my house. *Please* come, okay?"

"Maybe," I said.

"You're sad," she said. "I like sad boys."

Her sand-castle partner called out to her. She sprinted past him and dove into a collapsing wave. She'd written her address and "Come play with me" on a gum wrapper. She signed it *Dri.* "Is that a smiley face or a cross-eyed heart?" I said.

"Chuck it," John said.

"She's too pretty for me, right?"

"Too rich."

I watched her swim. The sky was clear, except for way out there, where the clouds were stacking up.

# 3

***SMALL CRAFT AND SURF ADVISORY: Expect steady rains for the next 48 hours. After the storm passes, strong winds will continue to make waters unpredictable.***

The storm beat up the beach for two days straight. The rains washed away the heat, and by late Tuesday afternoon the sky sparkled. Colors popped: the gold in the dune grass, the silver in the sand, the green in the sea. The waves were big as buildings, rising from far out. I watched them through the binoculars as they pounded the shore. I couldn't stop thinking about Dri's sand castle. "I have to go," I said.

"You really don't," John said.

"Maybe you'll meet someone."

"We're going home in two and a half weeks. The last thing I need is to start something with a spoiled rich girl who wants to go slumming."

"Everybody out here is from the city anyway."

"Not from our part of it. I'll end up working for these people someday. What happened to you? I thought you were Mr. I Like to Be Alone." A gust shook the trailer.

"I'll look like an idiot, standing around by myself."

"You'll look like an idiot either way. Matt, she'll rip the sweetness out of you, right through your rib cage. You'll never be able to squeeze it back in there. Look at him mope now." He chucked his study guide for the electrician's exam and grabbed a fresh T-shirt. "We're not staying late."

One of the lifeguards let us borrow his clunker. I tried not to be embarrassed as we pulled up to Dri's villa. The caretaker's cottage was twice as big as my house back in Queens, and the mansion itself was from a movie. The front door was open. The music was skin-shaking. Dudes in polos and button-downs hung out on the steps. John and I wore black tees. "Hope they don't think we're hit men," I said.

"Or waiters," John said. "If somebody hands me a dirty glass and asks for a refill, I'm out. I'm telling you, Matt, one hour, and then we go."

"I hear you."

"But you're not listening to me."

Somebody pointed us toward the buffet in the library. I served myself some turkey. John grabbed a cookie from a side table. He bit off an end and spit it up. "It's soap," he said. "Tell me that doesn't look like a Lorna Doone. Why do they have soap on a table?"

I stopped laughing long enough to say, "The *scent*, moron."

"Let's get out of here, Matt. Seriously."

"Hey!" JoJo swung his giant arms over our shoulders. "What's so funny?"

"Nothing, man," John said.

That got me laughing harder. JoJo laughed harder than I did.

"You don't even know why he's laughing," John said. John laughed now.

"I'll laugh at anything," JoJo said. "I'm thrilled you came. Dri prayed you would. 'Do you think my sad, sweet Matthew will come? *Do* you?' Or do you prefer we call you Matt?"

"Matt's good," I said.

"Is he, John?"

"He's an idiot," John said.

"Come." JoJo led us to the patio. Driana was the DJ. Her fingers tapped and swiped at two iPads. Her dreadlocks whipped across her face. Another girl hammered a laptop.

"I have to warn you about Dri," JoJo said. "She has a heart condition. It's too big. It gets her into trouble sometimes. You're not trouble, are you, Matt?"

"Not the kind you have to worry about."

"Then go to it." He pushed me toward the DJ table and pulled John away.

Dri screamed when she saw me. She hugged me. "I thoroughly soaked your shirt," she said. I was sweating plenty anyway. She smelled like vanilla soap. She yelled to her DJ partner, "Kris, sweetie, you have the table." She grabbed my hand and led me toward the cliff.

We walked barefoot along the beach. "I'm taking the year off," Dri said. She'd just graduated from Blessed Heart. It was the most expensive high school in the city and one of the most selective. You had to be supersmart to go there. Or superrich. She was still seventeen, almost eighteen. I had just turned seventeen. "In September I start work at animal control."

"The dog pound?" I had to yell, practically. The waves bombed the beach.

"Cats too. The odd potbellied pig. Ferrets, chickens."

"You're taking a year off to clean animal cages?"

"After that Harvard says I have to matriculate or reapply. Unless Daddy buys them another building. I'm messing with you, Matthew. I got in on my own steam, I swear."

"I don't doubt it."

"Most do, but thanks." She hip-checked me. "One of the dudes back at the party was like, 'You got into *Har*vard? Your dad's name is on the physics building, right?' "

"I'd never think that," I said.

"You're an awesome liar. Anyway, it's chemistry." She tickled me, and I tried not to flinch when she dug into the left side of my rib cage. "Not a building, though," she said. "An endowment. The Gonzaga Foundation for the Application of Scientific Solutions in Alleviating Poverty Throughout South America."

"Lot of words there."

"They do a lot," she said. "Vaccines, clean water, stuff like that."

"So you'll be president of that someday."

"I wanna be a vet." She was the rarest of kids my age: comfortable in her own skin. At ease with her money but not afraid to make fun of herself for it. Being around that balance of confidence and humility lit me up. She was plain cool. She was perfect.

"Where's your dog then?" I said.

Dri pouted. "She died. I'm rescuing another one when I get back in September." She took my water and saluted the stars. "To Sadie." She sipped and gave me the bottle. "I don't have cooties, promise."

"I don't care," I said.

"Then that worries me," she said. Again she tickled my left side, harder, and this time I did flinch. I sipped from the bottle. I guess it was sort of a kiss by proxy. I wondered if she wanted me to go the more direct route. "Sorry," I said. "About Sadie."

She wrinkled her nose and rubbed it on mine. "Let's go back. We have to save John from Stef. Do I need to tell you we Gonzaga girls are impulsive?"

"JoJo doesn't get mad?"

"Nothing bothers him. I know, he's crazy. And Stef draws the line at a three-second kiss. After that she feels bad and runs home to JoJo. She needs people to need her. You're too cute when you're sad. Ha, now you don't know what to do, do you?"

"John would never go behind somebody's back anyway."

"If you say so."

"Meaning?"

"No, I mean I'm sure he's cool," she said.

"How come you don't have a boyfriend?"

"Maybe I've been waiting for a nice boy to give me an ice cream. Hey, you have freckles. And yes, you should kiss me now, by the way."

I was about to when her phone roared like a lion. "Uh-oh," she said. "Daddy?"

# 4

The police cleared the house after a fight. John, JoJo, and I were in the kitchen with Dri. She was on the phone with her dad, who was in London for a business deal. "Nobody drank, Dad. Not here anyway." She covered the phone. "Matthew, one more minute."

"Say good night, Matt," John said.

"It's not even ten o'clock," JoJo said.

"We have to work tomorrow," John said.

"Come on now," JoJo said. "I'm sick of all these Hamptons people. You guys are—I forget the word in English."

"Normal?" John said.

JoJo put two massive hands on John's shoulders. "You like cars, right? They just got the new Porsche." He led us into the garage. It was a showroom. John asked if he could see the Porsche's engine.

"I only know how to drive it," JoJo said. "How do you pop the hood?"

John knew. He went on and on, explaining how beautiful the whole thing was. I couldn't have cared less about it. "I'm gonna see how Dri's doing," I said.

That snapped John out of his car craze. "Matt, we gotta go."

"Let's say bye at least."

JoJo hit the intercom. "Driana, somebody misses you."

*"Is Stef with you guys?"*

We met Dri on the terrace. "Her phone goes straight to voicemail," she said. We split up to cover the property. At the top of the stairs that led to the beach Dri and I found Stef's phone, along with her jeans. Dri called JoJo on the way down. "I think she wasn't kidding this morning when she said she wanted to go night surfing. Yes, I'm serious. I'm totally going to murder her." We ran a few hundred yards along the beach toward a mansion five or six houses down from Dri's. "My neighbor lets us borrow his boards," she said. "I swear, Matthew, I'm sending her back to Rio tomorrow morning."

A storage garage was built into the cliff. Dri ran her hand on top of the doorframe. "The key's always right here," she said. She checked the doormat; no luck.

"Want me to run up to the house and ask your neighbor to open it for us?" I said.

"He's in the city, I'm sure. His wife is pregnant and about to deliver any day." She hissed a string of words I didn't understand.

"Was that Portuguese?" I said.

"French. My mom says it's more polite for cursing."

By now JoJo and John were with us. "The key's in the doorknob," John said.

Dri blushed, more mad than embarrassed, I think. She pushed in and counted the surfboards. "Okay, thank God," she said. "They're all here."

JoJo pointed to an empty rack on the other side of the garage. "But the Windsurfer isn't," he said.

We followed Dri to the water's edge. The moon was high and bright, but seeing past the waves was a trick.

"She'll be okay," JoJo said. I don't think he believed himself. "She wins competitions all the time."

After a minute, John pointed her out. She ripped the crest of a wave. The wind was blowing offshore, from the northwest. Stef rode it south out to sea. "Call the police," John said.

"After what happened at the party they'll kill me," Dri said. "My father will kill me. I'm gonna kill her. Stef, get back here!"

Not that Stef would have listened, but she was out of hearing range.

"Dri, keep her in your sights," JoJo said. "Guys, can you give me a hand?"

We followed him up the beach to the storage garage. He pulled a tarp off a fiberglass boat with a shallow hull, maybe twenty feet long. Two cabinets doubled as benches along its sides. The boat was on a trailer, but the tires were flat.

"This is a really bad idea," John said.

"Please, guys, just help me get it down to the water?" JoJo said.

We slid the boat off the trailer. JoJo dragged it by its towrope. John and I pushed from the back. John grabbed the tarp on the way out. "She'll be cold," he said.

The garage doors spring-locked. They clapped shut behind us and sealed our fate. If they'd stayed open, maybe someone would have noticed a lot sooner that the boat was missing.

We muscled the boat over the sand, down to Dri. John sized up the ocean and the boat. "It isn't made for this kind of water," he said.

"Yes, it is," Dri said. "It's built to get out over the waves. It's a ship-to-shore boat. You use it to ferry people to and from their yachts."

"It doesn't even have a light on it," John said. "No radio either. I'm telling you, call the cops."

"I just did, okay?" Dri said. "While you guys were getting the boat. They told me it'll be twenty minutes before they can get a car out here."

"We need a helicopter," I said.

"They have to verify that it's not a crank call before they send a helicopter, they said." Dri climbed into the boat.

JoJo followed. “Guys, one last favor. Can you push us out as far as you can? I want to be sure the propeller clears the sand.”

John and I shouldered the boat into chest-high water. I pulled myself into it.

“No way, Matt,” John said.

“Matthew, really, stay here,” Dri said.

“You might need help,” I said.

“With what?” John said. “This isn’t your problem. Matt, don’t do it.”

JoJo started the engine. “Matt, please, get out. We’re losing her.”

“Then let’s go,” I said.

JoJo revved the throttle. John grabbed the side of the boat and climbed in. The boat punched into a wave, and we were airborne.

Five of us went out on the water that night. None of us came back whole, and not all of us came back.

# 5

I found out later the wind that night was forty miles an hour with gusts up to fifty. That's strong enough to knock you over. It's also a windsurfer's dream.

Stef was way out there where the surfing was fastest. The waves were just as big as the breakers closer to shore, but their peaks weren't sharp. We drove up and down black mountains of water to chase her. She was flying, and JoJo had the boat going full out to keep pace with her. It wasn't much of a boat. It didn't even have a wheel. The tiller was mounted to an older-looking outboard motor.

"It doesn't sound right," John said. "The engine. Was it tuned up this season?"

"Have no idea," Dri said.

"Your neighbor's a millionaire, and he's not smart enough to keep his boat in shape?" John said.

"Forgive me for not keeping track of his maintenance schedule," Dri said.

"JoJo, don't push it so hard. It's straining. Do we have a flashlight?" John nudged me off the bench seat and flipped it up. We found life vests, two short-arm paddles, a plastic milk crate filled with rope, binoculars, a bent screwdriver, a wrench kit and a rusty hammer, and a long-dead muskrat. Even in all that wind the funk was bad. I chucked it.

Dri checked under the other bench. She held up a heavy-duty flashlight.

"Spot her with it," John said. "She'll think the cops are after her and stop."

Dri yelled over the engine noise. "Knowing Stef, I bet she'll try to get away."

"Don't argue," John said. "Do it."

Dri eyed John. She clicked the switch. The flashlight was dead.

"JoJo," John said, "easy on the engine."

"I heard you the first time, John. Relax."

But John was relaxed, the only one who was. His words were harsh, but his eyes were easy, like he'd woken up from a nothing-special dream to a nothing-special life. He was too calm, I thought, just like he was the night his dad was murdered.

The boat's nose smacked an upslope. The wind and spray were cold. Ten minutes later we closed in on Stef. She whooped to us as she ramped off the top of a wave. She dropped behind it and disappeared.

We followed her over the wave. We'd been tracking her by the Windsurfer's light blue sail but now it was gone. We rode over the next wave and the next. She'd vanished, like we'd been chasing a ghost who'd suddenly grown tired of us.

"Go back," John said. "She must've fallen."

JoJo turned the boat back. The land was a thin black bar. We were farther out than I'd thought. The wind tore at our skin. My cheeks and ears burned. The engine screeched as the boat fought the waves. John edged JoJo away from the tiller. He slowed the boat until the engine noise smoothed out.

"There," Dri said.

"Where?" JoJo said.

Dri pointed to a shadow against a backdrop of moonlit water, but by now I had found Stef too, by her screaming. Her sail was down. She was trying to lift it, but the wind kept knocking it over. She yelled to us in Portuguese. I didn't need a translation to know she was saying hurry up. Another silhouette was in the water, but this one was circling the windsurf board. Then it stopped circling and charged Stef.

# 6

JoJo grabbed the tiller from John. He rushed the boat at the fin, but the shark didn't back off. It zeroed in on Stef until it was an arm's length from her. The moon lit up her tear tracks, but more than crying she was laughing. *"É um golfinho,"* she said.

JoJo and Dri cheered, and John and I looked at each other like, Are these people insane?

JoJo hugged me so hard my ribs ached. "It's a dolphin," he said.

I tapped my phone's flashlight app. It wasn't the spotlight we needed before, but it threw enough light to catch the reflection of the dolphin's eye. On TV they're gray and tame. This one was glossy black with silver- and honey-colored spots. It was bigger than I would have thought, and much more powerful looking.

"It's protecting her from the sharks," JoJo said. He took a picture of Stef. *Click*, flash. The dolphin backed away but not for long. It eased toward the boat for a closer look.

"How many years am I surfing, and never has a shark bothered me," Stef said. "That's why this *golfinho* girl here frightened me. Right, pretty girl?"

"So not cool, Stef," Dri said.

"The wind called me out here, Dri. The sky—my God, the sky will never be like this again. Don't you see it?" She spoke in Portuguese to JoJo and he laughed and nodded, and then Stef went back to English. "Guys, don't let your anger blind you. Look up, just for a second, and then you can return to being as mad at me as you want. We're in a temple. Let's just be peaceful in the temple for a minute, okay?"

I looked up. The sky was more stars than black. It sparkled pink, green, light blue. My anger drained into the wind—a little bit. My cheeks weren't so hot anymore. Even John seemed mesmerized.

"We are so lucky," JoJo said. "To get to see *this*? God loves us. Truly we are loved."

Dri was looking up too, smiling, and then she frowned, as if remembering she was supposed to be furious. "Stef, if you're not in the boat in ten seconds I swear I'm locking you in your room for the rest of the summer, and I'm totally telling your dad you put all our lives at risk."

"How about you, pretty one?" Stef said to John. "Are you happy you came along? He doesn't answer. Yes, I'm talking to you. What is his name again? John, right? I'm kidding, John. I know you, and

I love you, I think. You too, Matthew, even though you don't know where Rio is. Thank you for being out here with us. We're friends now. We're of one blood, okay? Blessed together in the temple."

"Stef!" Dri said.

"Hold your jets," Stef said, treading toward the boat, dragging the Windsurfer.

"Cool your jets," Dri said. "Hold your horses."

"That's what we should do tomorrow. Ride horses on the beach! John, do you like horses?"

"I'd like to go home," John said.

"Only you, my angel," she said to JoJo. "Only you understand. Sorry, I needed to fly a little."

"You need to stop being selfish," Dri said. She knelt down and leaned out of the boat, extending her hand toward Stef.

"Driana, she apologized," JoJo said. "We had an adventure with no harm done. We have all that pizza left from the party. We'll go home and tell stories about what happened and make it even more grand than it really was. Than it *is.* Yes, this is a one-time sky."

Dri, John, and I reached down to pull Stef into the boat.

"Wait, let me say good-bye to my friend." Stef tried to give the dolphin a one-armed hug. It bucked, and its tail kicked up into the Windsurfer. The board twirled out of the water. Stef had never let go of the board. She'd been gripping it by the toehold the whole time. Maybe I only imagined I heard the bones crack, but her arm from her elbow down was facing the wrong way, and a slick red bone tip pierced her skin. She groaned. Her eyes rolled back and her head slipped beneath the surface.

Dri dove and broke the surface without a splash. An eerie sucking noise followed Dri into the water as the surface healed itself where she had ripped a hole into it. I dove after her, remembering to kick off my sandals but not to leave my phone. I lost it as I hit the water. The flashlight app was still on and the light was dropping away too fast, spinning into the darkness below me. The dolphin chased the fading blinks.

I lifted Stef's head from the water. Her eyes were open, but she was unconscious. "Her head's bleeding," I said. "I think maybe the surfboard fin clipped it."

Dri and I found the cut by feel. It was behind Stef's hairline, at the base of her skull. At one end of the cut the skin flapped.

"Stef, wake up," Dri said. "C'mon now, don't do this."

"Don't shake her," I said. I dragged Stef to the boat with the lifeguard crawl. JoJo and John grabbed her. "Easy," I said. "She hit her head. Keep her neck straight."

JoJo didn't listen. He yanked her into the boat. I pulled myself up and in. We laid Stef out on the slippery floor. She wasn't breathing.

I had done rescue breathing in my first responder course exactly once, and that was on a mannequin. The boat rocked as Dri pulled herself up and in. I tilted Stef's head back to open her airway. If her spinal cord was damaged, I'd just made it worse, but what other choice did I have? I clamped her nose and put my mouth over hers and tried to breathe into her lungs.

This was crazy, trying to breathe into a real live human being. Everything I'd learned over the summer in the CFR class was gone. My memory was shot. I couldn't get any air into her lungs. She still had a pulse, though. I felt it in her neck.

"Hurry, Matt, please," JoJo said.

I didn't know what to do, except to try again. I repositioned her head to open her airway, and this time when I breathed into her mouth she coughed salt water into mine. She sucked at the air.

"Oh my God, Matthew, thank you," Dri said. JoJo slapped my shoulders, more like pounded them.

"Matt," John said. He pointed to the dark, shiny puddle spreading underneath Stef. Blood pulsed from the rip in her arm. I applied pressure to the artery with my fingertips, and then more pressure, and it still bled. It wasn't spurting and spraying, but it wasn't trickling either. Stef was somewhere between unconscious and slightly aware of the pain I was inflicting as I was clamping her artery. She moaned and tried to pull my fingers from her arm. JoJo held her down. "I saw a towel in the cabinet," I said. "Somebody rip a strip for me?"

JoJo jumped and went to the wrong cabinet and rocked the boat hard in the process. John moved at half speed to the right cabinet and ripped me a strip. I forced myself to slow down as I tied the strip around Stef's arm just above the wound.

"That's right, Matt," John said. "Nice and easy."

I twisted the knot until the blood flow stopped. If we didn't get her to a hospital within a couple of hours she would lose the arm, I was pretty sure. At least that's what my books said. I was supposed to write TK, shorthand for tourniquet, on her forehead in Sharpie ink, along with the time I'd tied off the blood flow to the injured limb. This way when the medics rushed her into the ER and handed her off to the nurses and then they handed her off to the doctors, who would hand her off to the surgeons, everybody at the hospital would know her arm didn't have any blood circulating to it for a while. We had a better chance of finding another dead muskrat in the cabinets before we found a Sharpie. I went to mark the time on my phone, until I remembered I'd fed it to the dolphin. "John, mark the time," I said.

But he'd already done it. He showed me his phone display. The time was ticking down on his stopwatch, from sixty minutes to zero. I'd made him quiz me on this stuff the nights before I had a test. We were already into T-minus fifty-seven minutes. I looked to the shore. We were really far out now. I couldn't see us getting from where we were to a hospital in less than fifty-seven minutes. The problem with a tourniquet is, once you apply it only a doctor can undo it. The surgeon closes the wound first and then eases the blood into the limb. If you turned the blood back on full blast, you might blow apart the damaged blood vessels or infect them or something like that—I couldn't remember. My heart ached with all the things I didn't know. All I knew was I couldn't take off the tourniquet. I bandaged Stef's head with strips of towel.

"She's okay, Matthew?" Dri said.

I had no idea, but I said, "She'll be okay until we get her to the hospital."

"Matt, you are my friend forever." JoJo clapped my shoulder with even more enthusiasm this time. He almost knocked me over. He quick-stepped to the engine and revved the throttle. The boat jerked and threw us to the floor. The engine hiccupped and sputtered out, and all we heard was the wind.

JoJo tried the ignition. Nothing. Then John tried and the engine screeched. John unscrewed the gas cap and looked in. "Yup," he said. "We're empty."

Dri, John, and JoJo took out their phones. Dri's was wet and wouldn't turn on. John frowned at his. JoJo shook his head.

# 7

Dri flipped up the bench seat and reached into the cabinet. She lifted a gallon jug and sniffed the funnel top. “Beautiful,” she said. “I thought it was water when I saw it before.”

“The giveaway was the funnel top,” John said.

“John, can you not be snide for half a minute?” Dri’s eyes were glossy. She looked to JoJo for support, but he was comforting Stef, trying to. She was unconscious now, and I was relieved, a little bit anyway. I dreaded what she would do when she woke up to find her arm torn open and turning gray.

John nodded at the gas jug. “Let me see if it’s still good,” he said.

“Gas goes bad?” Dri said.

“That muskrat was dead a while. When was the last time your neighbor got the boat out? Oh right, you have no idea. Awesome. Okay, then when was the last time you borrowed it?”

“Last summer? No, the summer before, I think.”

"With those flat tires on the trailer, you probably were the last one to use it too." John sniffed the jug. He shrugged and poured gas into the tank. He tried the ignition. The engine shrieked. "There's air in the line," he said. He turned on his phone flashlight and lit up the engine housing.

"Are you getting a signal now?" JoJo said, shaking his own phone like that would kick in a satellite connection.

John either didn't hear him or ignored him. "Get me that wrench kit from the cabinet," he said to me. "I saw it in the bottom of the milk crate. Bring the hammer too."

I brought him the tools. "I should grab the surfboard," I said. "For Stef. To stabilize her spine."

"I have no idea what you're talking about," John said.

"I want to use it as a—"

"I don't care why, just get it done."

The ocean was warmer than the air, but I didn't love swimming away from the boat in that dark water. I swam fast. A glittery shadow appeared to my left, just beneath the surface. The dolphin was swimming alongside me, not too close but way too close for comfort. I pulled myself onto the surfboard and paddled hard for the boat. The sail was heavy and dragged in the water, but JoJo plucked the rig from the sea—mast, surfboard, and all—like it weighed about as much as an inflatable pool toy.

We broke the fin off the board and disconnected the mast, and then we lashed Stef to the board with the sail. She was a mummy except for her head and feet. I tied her head down to the board with another strip of towel. When she came to—if she came to—she would scream. Being pinned like that is scary. They made us do it to each other in the first responder class. There was one time before that too, when I was pinned down, but I couldn't think about that now.

"Matt?" Dri said. "I'm sorry."

I was too. I knew enough first aid to know I didn't know enough. "She'll be okay," I said. Even then I knew I was lying. Stef had a concussion for sure. The doctors would need to drill her head to relieve the pressure building in her skull. We'd be lucky to get her to a hospital by morning.

JoJo's clothes were dry, but he shivered with Dri. My teeth chattered. John was the only one who wasn't cold. His hands were steady as he took apart the engine. Dri and I stripped off our wet clothes to our underwear. We huddled Stef, one of us on each side, to share body heat. JoJo laid the tarp over us.

"I need somebody to hold the light for me," John said. JoJo helped him.

The tarp kept the chill away a little bit. At least it kept the wind off our skin. I felt Dri's fingertips on the left side of my rib cage. She traced the scalpel line that ran down my left side from my armpit to my hip. "What happened?" she said.

I was thinking how I should respond, if I should respond. I stared into the sky, like maybe the stars would spell out a half-decent answer for me, or any answer at all. I still wasn't sure what had happened myself, but the parts that I remembered . . . well, I didn't want to remember them. Even in the moonlight the Milky Way stood out sharply. It stood on its end like it was about to tip over. Stef saved me when she moaned.

"It's okay, sweetheart," Dri said.

It wasn't even close to okay. Stef began to scream. She wailed on and on in Portuguese.

"She wants to know why we tied her up," Dri said. "She says her arm is on fire."

# 8

*Wednesday, August 18, midnight, day one . . .*

Stef's screaming turned to gagging. She was going to choke on her vomit. JoJo and I rolled her onto her side, which wasn't easy since she was tied to the windsurf board. JoJo balanced it on its edge while Stef vomited bile for what seemed too long a time. Dri used her wet shirt to clean up Stef's face.

John didn't even look our way. He was breaking down the engine to its parts. A bolt rolled over the floor of the boat, back and forth with the waves.

Seeing that bolt, I realized that all the rocking was making me dizzy. Between the waves and the wind we were getting batted around pretty good. I thought maybe I was going to throw up too. It was hitting me full force now: We were out in the Atlantic Ocean in the middle of the night, in choppy water, with a seriously injured woman. Even in that cramped boat with four other people, I'd never felt so alone.

Dri huddled with Stef underneath the tarp. After a bit Stef stopped squirming. Her eyes fluttered and she seemed dazed.

JoJo took off his shirt and gave it to me. "To keep you warm," he said, but I knew he'd seen the long line that scarred my left side. He stared a little too hard into my eyes and forced a smile. I traded places with him and held the phone light for John. I'd wrung out my jeans but they were still too wet to wear, and I felt like an idiot without any pants on, in black underwear too. They might as well have said MADE IN NYC on them. "She'll die if we don't get her to an emergency room," I said.

"She'll die anyway," John said. "Hand me the screwdriver, the flat head."

"You don't think you'll have it running by morning?" I said.

"Matt, look at the horizon."

"Where?"

"Everywhere. Do you see any land?"

I didn't. The wind hadn't let up. It pushed us farther out to sea. "We still have to be in an area of recreational boat traffic," I said. "We'll cross paths with somebody."

"Sure," John said. "Who wouldn't want to be out on the ocean in a windstorm at two in the morning?"

"I couldn't help myself."

"What?"

"She's beautiful. She was holding my hand. How do you let go? You don't. You can't. John, I'm sorry."

"Save your apology for my mother."

"Then why'd you climb aboard?"

"Shut up and hold the light steady."

By three a.m. the moon closed in on the horizon. Stef moaned between coughs. Dri whispered into Stef's ear. She kissed her forehead and stroked her cheek.

John disconnected a tube from the engine block. He sucked gas from the line and spit it overboard.

"Fixed?" JoJo clapped John's back.

John definitely ignored him this time. He reattached the tube. We helped him reassemble the engine. Half an hour later he turned the ignition switch. The engine roared. We cheered, until John turned off the engine.

"What are you doing?" Dri said.

"We don't have enough fuel to make it back," John said.

"How do you know?"

"We have a gallon of gas. This kind of engine burns ten gallons an hour, I figure. That's six minutes of drive time. At top speed we'll get four miles before the engine conks out. That's without a head wind. We're at least fifteen miles offshore by now. Maybe twenty, maybe more."

"We have to try," Dri said.

"Which way do you want to go?" John said. "Where's land?"

"Why'd you bother to fix the engine if all we're going to do is drift?" Dri said.

"If we see a boat, it won't see us," John said. "Especially at night without any lights. Even in the daytime, we'll be too low in the water. We'll have to chase any ship we see and hope we get close enough that it spots us."

JoJo checked his phone again for a signal.

"If you can't see land, you won't get a signal," John said.

"I was two hundred miles offshore last summer. I had a signal the whole time."

"You were on a yacht, right?" John said. "They have satellite uplinks. Once you're a couple of miles offshore, a regular cell phone is useless."

"But Dri got off a call to the police right before we went out on the water," I said. "Dri, you said they would be there in twenty minutes, right?"

"We were too far offshore for them to see us by then," John said.

"Okay," I said, "but the cops would have tried to talk to somebody before they left. They rang the front bell, and nobody answered. Then they probably tried Dri's phone and got her voicemail."

"And figured it was a crank call," John said.

"But they're going to check with the caretaker, to be sure," I said.

"They're only there in the off-season," Dri said.

"They take care of your mansion for you all year and you get rid of them for the summer, huh?" John said. "Nice."

"It is, actually. They're down in Brazil at my uncle's for an extended ski vacation. The next person coming over is Antonia, to clean the house."

"In the morning, yes?" JoJo said.

"Thursday morning, though." That was about thirty hours away.

"Brian will wonder why we didn't bring his car back," I said. "And our bosses. Neither of us was late for work all summer. When we don't show up this morning, they'll know something's wrong. They'll try to call us, then the hospitals, then the cops."

"None of them had any idea where we were headed last night, Matt. The earliest anybody will start looking for us is Thursday morning, and even that's a long shot. Why would the maid or whoever think to call the cops? Are you home every time she's there?"

"No," Dri said, "but I'd never leave the house a mess for her the way it is now, after the party. She'll see a random car parked in the driveway. She'll know something's wrong. She'll try to call me. She'll call my dad. He'll try to call me. When I don't get back to him, he'll call the police."

"After how long?" John said.

"A day?"

"Now we're into Friday," John said. "And then what? Why would anybody think we're out on the water?"

"We'll run into another boat today," JoJo said. "For sure."

"On our way over to your house, the radio kept saying it over and over," John said. "The rough seas warning is being extended another forty-eight hours. You know, the warning that kept all the boaters off the water last night. At least the ones with any brains."

"This isn't helping," Dri said. "Being negative."

"I'm being realistic."

Stef moaned and JoJo comforted her. He spoke softly in Portuguese and made her hold his hand.

"JoJo, you have the flashlight app too," Dri said.

"It won't work," John said. "You think you're going to flag down a boat with a weak little phone light?"

"If you'd let me finish, I was going to say that the flashlight app has a strobe effect. You can program it. My friend Kristie was using it when we were DJ-ing last night. We can program it with S-O-S."

"So you want to randomly flash S-O-S north, south, east, west and hope to get lucky?" John said. "That app will burn out the phone fast. We have to save the battery for when we need it. If we see a ship, and we get close enough where it has a shot of picking up the light, that's when we activate the SOS."

"So, we're just going to float around out here for the next few days and wait to die?" Dri said.

"It'll take more than a few days, unfortunately," John said.

Dri moved closer to John, out of Stef's hearing range. "But what about Stef?"

"Nobody told her to get on that Windsurfer," John said.

"Why do you have to be like this?" Dri said. "You don't think she feels bad about this?"

"She feels bad all right, but not about this," John said.

"My uncle adopted her, John. From a rough part of the *favela*. The slum."

"That gives her a free pass to act like an idiot?"

"You know about the Rio slums?"

"Do you?" John said.

"John, be cool," I said, except he was. His words and face didn't match. He looked perfectly relaxed.

"Her mother was gunned down in front of her," Dri said. "A drug deal went bad and Stef's mom was hit in the cross fire."

"So what?" John said.

"Are you serious? Stef was holding her when she bled out. She was five years old, and she remembers it like it was yesterday."

"Spare me, okay? So she's a head case. If she had a death wish, going out into the deep water at night, that's her business. But now she's pulling down the four of us with her. You yourself called her selfish."

"You didn't have to get on the boat, John," Dri said.

"Yes, I did." John looked my way, and then he looked away.

# 9

*Sunrise . . .*

Stef's arm was a prop from a zombie movie. The skin was green and purple and gray where it had ripped. She wet herself with dark urine. I remembered reading about this, how it could happen after a major trauma. I couldn't remember specifically what the dark color meant. Something with the kidneys or liver or both or neither. Whatever was happening inside her body, I was sure I couldn't fix it. I felt like a fraud, acting as the ship's doctor, but I was the closest thing we had to medically trained personnel.

I swore I'd get some actual hands-on training when we got back to land. Supervised training, with people who'd gotten their hands bloody more than once. This disaster with Stef was too much of a crash course. It was like the Spanish I learned in junior high: I memorized enough to get good grades on the exams, and then I knew nothing out on the street, until I just threw myself into real live conversations and made tons of mistakes and braved a lot of laughter. We didn't have room for any more mistakes out here in the Atlantic, and I couldn't imagine any of us would be laughing anytime soon. I palmed Stef's forehead. Her skin was hot, and she shivered nonstop. Dri huddled up next to Stef in the front of the boat and caressed Stef's cheek.

JoJo took the lookout post on the right side of the boat. I took the left side, and John looked off the back. Real sailors would describe the positions as starboard, port, and stern. I picked up the terms when Mr. Owen made us read an abridged version of *Moby-Dick* in ninth grade. Beyond that, I didn't know anything about boating. None of us did. We didn't know anything about one another either. Not really, not yet. We were from the Upper East Side of Manhattan, the Copacabana district of Rio de Janeiro, and Woodhull, Queens. And here we were facing death together in a hundred square feet of boat. Even John was a stranger to me. I was used to his coolness, but he was all-cold now. I'd seen him this way only once before, when his father's blood spattered my face. He was a stranger to me that time too.

"We'll run into someone soon," Dri said.

"We will," JoJo said. "The universe provides."

John frowned, and I read his mind. *For some people, the universe provides. The rest of us scramble.*

By now we'd been out on the water for eight hours. That's a long time in a stalled boat. The water was desolate, the sky was cloudless, deep blue, and the wind was steady, strong, and dry. Rain was not on the way. I'd gotten my wish. I was in the desert. By midmorning the glare blinded us, and I felt like somebody had drilled two-inch screws into my eyes.

Dri and JoJo took turns comforting Stef, or trying to. John and I rotated watch duties every few minutes with Dri or JoJo, two on lookout, one on break. I closed my eyes and the sun still shined. I tried not to think about the fact that a human being can't go without water more than a few days. But we'd be rescued by then, I was pretty sure. As sure as I was that Stef was a goner if the rescue didn't happen by tomorrow. Dri had the hardest job, lying to Stef and maybe to herself.

"Why can't I feel my arm?" Stef said.

"You broke it, Stef. Your brain blocks the nerve signals to spare you the pain."

"How bad is it?"

"You'll need surgery."

"Will I be able to surf again?"

"You will."

"Why won't you let me look at it?"

"Because Matthew wrapped it up nice and tight to keep it clean," Dri said.

Those strips of towel were in no way keeping the wound clean.

I'd wrapped the arm so Stef couldn't see it. So we wouldn't have to look at it.

"Why am I tied down?"

"We have to keep you still, Stef."

"I have to go the bathroom."

"Just go, sweetheart."

"I really have to go."

"I'll clean you up. It's okay."

"Just untie me. Please. I'll scream! Why can't I feel my arm?" The same conversation over and over. JoJo left his watch post to comfort Stef.

"Matt," John said. "You're up. JoJo, give him the binoculars."

# 10

*Midafternoon . . .*

The sun burned through our clothes. My arms and face were dark after a summer out in the sun, but I had been careful to cover my shoulders. We couldn't afford to get sun poisoning out here. The blisters would break and become infected.

I dipped into the ocean to cool off. I kept my clothes on to keep from being burned. I hung on to the towrope and tried to make my body go limp in the water on the shady side of the boat. I couldn't quite get myself to let go of the tension in my neck, my jaw, my stomach. I wasn't as thirsty, though, in the water. It felt cooler way out here, however many miles we were from shore, and some spots were plain cold. After ten minutes I actually started to shiver, and I made myself climb back into the boat and face the situation with

Stef. There was no avoiding her. She was laid out in the middle of the boat.

Within ten minutes my clothes were dry, even my jeans. I couldn't remember a day with less humidity. The water had flattened out some, but the wind was as steady as it had been all night. I cupped my hands around my eyes to shade them from the glare coming off the water, and I looked up. The afternoon sky had turned a blue I'd never seen before, except in a computer-generated image, the kind you find in a sci-fi movie where the good guys escape to a perfect world. Most of the sky was clear, but even the one cloudy part was beautiful. The clouds looked like lace. This would have been the best beach day of the summer if we were on land. If Dri were caressing my face instead of Stef's.

"Thirsty," Stef said.

Dri rinsed the gas jug and filled it halfway with salt water.

"She can't drink that," I said.

"I'm going to distill it," Dri said. She set the jug on its side. "The idea is the water evaporates. It leaves the salt behind. The droplets condense on the inside top of the jug and drip out the nozzle." She found a peanut can in the cabinet. The muskrat did us the favor of emptying it. Dri set it under the nozzle.

"Where'd you learn this?" I said.

"Last summer I volunteered with my father's foundation," she said. "Before they let me go into the rain forest with them, they made me take a survival class. We did it with muddy river water, to try to get the sediment out of it. It sort of worked, but they said it would work even better with salt water."

"Cool," I said. It was, until we hit a pair of waves broadside. The boat rocked and the water sloshed around the container. It wasn't long before the nozzle started to drip, but the drops that came out tasted more like salt water than fresh.

"Nope," Dri said. "It's no good."

"Just a sip," Stef said. "Please, Dri."

"No way, Stef. For every sip of salt water, you pee two."

"So?"

Dri wet Stef's lips with her fingertip. We rigged the tarp to shade her. The wind cooled the air under there a little, but it was still oven-like. We took turns fanning Stef and nodding off in the hot gloom. "Thirsty," Stef whispered. "Thirsty."

"Can you guys cut me a piece of tarp?" Dri said. "Say four-foot square?"

JoJo and I stretched a section of it over the top edge of the boat's side. John scored the tarp with the flat-head screwdriver. The tarp was plastic-coated canvas. To cut what we needed took twenty minutes that felt like two hundred under that sun.

Dri emptied the wrenches and rope and hammer from the plastic milk crate, and then she lined the crate with the patch of tarp we'd just cut to form a sort of bowl. She poured in an inch of seawater. She put the peanut can in the middle of the bowl. To keep the can from floating she weighed it down with a wrench.

She stretched a flap of tarp over the top of the crate and tied it down with an elastic cord from the hem of JoJo's sweatshirt. She placed a dead flashlight battery on top of the tarp, directly over the peanut can. The top of the tarp, which was dark green, sank a little where the battery weighed it down.

"Dark colors absorb light and heat," Dri said. "That seawater is going to get hot fast. When you put plastic wrap over a bowl of hot soup, you see the steam condense into droplets on the plastic, right? If you press your finger down into the plastic, the droplets will run toward that spot, the way the droplets in our little distiller setup here are going to run toward the depression the battery is making in the tarp. They'll condense into bigger drops until they drip."

"Except the peanut can is going to catch the drops," I said. "You're awesome."

We leaned back to let the sun bake the box. John studied the setup and nodded.

"Do I take that as a compliment?" Dri said.

"Even if it doesn't work, it's reasonable," he said.

"*Rea*sonable," Dri said. "Gee, thanks."

"It's a solid try." John went back to his watch post.

JoJo kissed Dri's forehead. "Would it be unreasonable of me to call you a genius?"

I nodded at the box. "How long?"

"Let's check in an hour, if we're not rescued by then." She squeezed my hand. "Thank you," she said.

"Thank *you*," I said.

She smiled. "You're crazy."

"Hey," John said. "Check it out." He pointed toward the horizon. I didn't see anything until he gave me the binoculars. It was a sailboat, a big one, with two masts, but it was sailing away from us. In ten minutes it was gone from view.

"Guys, wait," JoJo said, pointing to the opposite side of the ocean. He had the binoculars now. He handed them back to me. A speedboat was flying full out.

"How far away, you figure?" I said. I handed John the binoculars.

"I'd say two miles. We'll never catch it." He nodded to JoJo. "Try."

JoJo flashed the SOS. The boat zipped toward the horizon and out of sight.

"Even if they saw it," John said, "it's just one of a billion glints on the waves."

Dri tapped up JoJo's compass app, but it didn't work. "John, let me borrow your wristwatch," she said. She pointed the hour hand of John's Timex at the sun. "Midway between the hour hand and noon on the dial is south." We looked down into the water. Faint wake lines trailed the boat. They pointed southeast, out into the

Atlantic. "I was hoping the wind had shifted and we were blowing west toward land."

"Or at least some commercial boat traffic," I said. "The watch trick. Survival class?"

"They dumped us into the middle of the woods with nothing but a wristwatch and told us to find our way out," Dri said. "Why do you think we're not headed for commercial boat traffic?"

"I haven't seen any birds all day." I pointed for her to look into the water on the shady side of the boat. There wasn't any glare and you could see down pretty deep. "I haven't seen any fish either."

Dri nodded. "No birds, no fish, no fishing boats."

"You guys?" Stef said. Her voice startled us. Except for a little moaning she'd been quiet the last few hours. "Don't hate me," she said. "Please don't."

"We love you, Stef," Dri said.

JoJo spoke to her in Portuguese, and I kept hearing the word *amor.*

"Where's John?" Stef said. "Please, I have to talk with him. John? I'm so sorry. JoJo, please, make him understand I didn't mean for this to happen." Then she spoke to JoJo in Portuguese.

"She says she wanted to get to know you," JoJo said. "She feels a kinship with you, John, yet she doesn't know why."

John stared at her. He nodded the slightest bit, more to himself than Stef, I think. His eyes caught mine, and then he went back to his watch post.

"Will you take the picture today, Jo?" Stef said. "Make it John and Matt. Make John smile."

"She takes a picture to commemorate every day," JoJo said. "You know, an image that defines what that day was about for her."

"Please?" Stef said.

I stood next to John. He didn't smile. JoJo took a picture. John got back to his binoculars. Dri and JoJo cornered John in his watch post, out of Stef's earshot.

"You can't acknowledge her, John?" Dri said.

"I'm acknowledging her," he said. "Or I'm acknowledging her pain anyway. I wouldn't wish it on anyone."

"Then can you let her know that?" Dri said.

John kept his voice low, so Stef couldn't hear. As soft as his voice was, the words came out hard. "What do you want me to say to her? That I feel bad for her? Like that's going to help her? My pity? It's only going to make her feel worse. She knows she made a stupid mistake, and there's nothing I can say to fix that."

"John, c'mon now, man," JoJo said. "Your grudge goes so deep?"

"I don't have a grudge against her. We are where we are, however we got here, and I'm dealing with it. The only thing I can do to help her is keep a lookout, and that's what I'm doing. Coddling her isn't going to save her or us."

“It costs you nothing to tell her not to worry, that it’s okay,” Dri said.

“It’s not okay,” John said. “She’s not okay. I’m not lying to her.” That was the one time he looked a little edgy out there. Stef had him pegged, and he didn’t like that at all. They did have something in common. Her mother and his father were gunned down. The difference was, Stef’s mom’s death was accidental. Mr. Costello was targeted.

“Spell me, Matt,” John said. “I have to rest my eyes.” He gave me the binoculars and slipped into the water.

# 11

*Late afternoon . . .*

Dri took the peanut can out of the water distiller box she had made from the tarp and milk crate. She sipped from the can. "Blehk. Tastes like hot plastic."

"Better that than salt," I said.

"It tastes like that too, a little, but it's not even close to as salty as ocean water. I actually think it might be working, our little distiller here."

"Your distiller," I said. "You saved us."

"Don't get too excited yet," Dri said. "Look."

John, JoJo, and I looked into the tin. After an hour of collecting evaporated water, it wasn't half-full. I could have emptied it in a gulp, and I wanted to. Dri held the water to Stef's lips. She drank most of it and spilled the rest when she started gagging. We rolled her onto her side and held her like that while she threw up. After she vomited the water she didn't have anything left in her stomach, but she dry heaved for a long time.

John didn't seem to notice Stef was hacking her guts out. He set up the distiller to catch another half cup of water before the sun went down. We had two hours before dark.

Dri slipped over the side of the boat into the water to clean herself up. She was the one who held Stef's head while she was throwing up. Stef had vomited into Dri's chest and neck and maybe her face, but Dri never flinched.

JoJo and I got Stef settled. She moaned in her sleep. "Matt," JoJo said, "I don't know if you should tell me what I want to hear or what I need to hear. Or is there any possibility they can be the same thing?"

"It'll be okay," I said.

"But will she? Will Stef lose her arm? I can't imagine the doctors will be able to fix it. It's turning gray, Matt." He hid his face in his sweatshirt collar. "I feel that this is my fault."

"It's not your fault," I said. "It's nobody's."

"It's *mine*." His eyes flashed when he pulled away his sweatshirt collar. "She told us yesterday morning that she was going out onto the water that night, and I didn't do anything but laugh, even after she said she was serious. I think this provoked her, you see? She saw my laughter as a dare.

"I've known her since we were ten years old, when she cut me in the line for the diving board at the club pool where our families were members. We were fast friends, best friends. I told her I loved her that same day we met, over a plate of french fries, and do you know what? I meant it. I just knew she was the person for me, or that I was born to be hers. Do you know what I mean? It was in her eyes, her smile, something I had not seen before. I don't know the words in English—or in Portuguese either. She just had magic about her, the kind you feel when you jump from a height, the top diving platform, you know? Except you never hit the water. You keep falling and screaming and laughing, terrified not so much of the fall as the fact that it must end. I pledged my love to her every day we hung out together after that first day too, and I meant it more each time. And then one day two years ago, when we were doing homework together, she said, 'Hey?' 'Yes, *meu amor*?' I said, figuring she wanted me to do her homework for her again. But she didn't at all. She said it back. She told me she loved me too. But I don't deserve to be with her now. I let her down. Promise me she'll be all right."

"We'll keep her as safe as we can until she gets to the hospital," I said. I tried not to look out at the horizon. We were the only living things in view.

"You can't promise me, can you?" JoJo said.

The best I could come up with was, "It'll all work out. You'll see."

He wasn't listening anyway. He kissed Stef's forehead. "If she hates me after this, I don't know what I'll do," he said. "Truly, without her I wouldn't be the same person. I couldn't possibly be. She defines me."

At dusk we spotted a tanker. It wasn't that far away, but it was moving too fast for us to catch it. Its wake lines were bigger than the waves. We flashed SOS with John's and JoJo's phones, but it kept going.

"How can they not stop?" JoJo said.

"The tankers are on autopilot this far out," John said. "Even if they saw us through the glare, they wouldn't be able to pick out the phone flashes from the flashes off the waves. There's no reason for them to think we're in trouble without something like a flare. And even if they did think we were in trouble, you know how much it costs in time lost and fuel to stop a ship like that and turn it off course? If we were in its way, it would have to run us down."

"Maybe they saw us and called in our position," Dri said.

"Sure," John said. He didn't bother tracking the ship anymore. He turned the binoculars to a different part of the ocean. It was empty all the way around except for that vanishing tanker. Just before the ship disappeared its stack blew reddish smoke. It hung on the horizon like blood spray.

The air turned cold quickly, even before the last bit of sun disappeared. In the opposite part of the sky the stars were already sharp. John and JoJo took the first watch while Dri and I tucked

Stef under the tarp. JoJo was reluctant to give up the job of comforting Stef. He spoke to her in Portuguese and pointed toward the back of the boat, where he was headed. Stef grunted and said, "I know," and from that I figured JoJo said he'd be right over there if Stef needed him, that she didn't need to worry. She didn't seem worried anyway, not anymore. She wasn't shivering as much, but her skin was cooler, bluer. Dri stroked Stef's cheek and whispered a lullaby to her.

I gave the two of them a little space and tried to get some rest in the front of the boat. There was no room to lie down, so I sat back against the wall and closed my eyes. I was too hungry to sleep anyway. Pretty soon Dri sat next to me. "She's asleep," she said.

I nodded. Stef looked more than asleep, nearer to comatose. Her face wasn't tight around the eyes and mouth the way it was until sunset.

Dri rested her head on my shoulder. Even though the situation we were in was crazy and horrible, I couldn't help but feel awed. The water, the sky, the way Dri's eyes caught the twilight and turned green-gold . . . the colors were surreal, movie-like. The moon was coming up and the ocean looked like the desert, wave after wave of shifting silvery dunes. "Ever see *Lawrence of Arabia*?" I said.

"It was one of those movies that everybody told me I had to see, but I just never got around to it. Was it good?"

"Perfect."

"A boy who likes old movies. Interesting. Most dudes your age are into *Grand Theft Auto*, no? Kill as many people as you can over four slices of pizza?"

"Not me. No way. I'm serious."

"I definitely see that," she said. "Anyway, that's good news for me."

"Why?"

She held my hand. "I read *Seven Pillars of Wisdom*," she said. "Hello, the book that *Lawrence of Arabia* was based on?"

I nodded, like of course I knew the movie was based on a book. "It was one of those books everybody told me I had to read—"

"—but you never got around to it, I know, I know."

"It's next on my TBR pile," I said. "Right after I finish Batman #368, *A Revenge of Rainbows*, Batman and Robin versus Crazy-Quilt."

"Why do you like it?" she said.

"Who doesn't like the Caped Crusader?"

"Don't make me pinch that freckled cheek a little too hard. It will smart. Seriously, what draws you to the Lawrence movie?"

"Dude escapes to the desert. What's not to like? My mom and dad have all these DVDs stockpiled from, like, twenty years of shopping the bargain bins. I've been putting them onto drives for them, to make space in the bookcases. I watch them sometimes, while I'm transferring them. Most of them were really good, but *Lawrence of*

*Arabia* stopped me cold. I don't know, you have to see it. Everything looks clean and quiet and wide open, like nobody's going to mess with you out there."

"Ever been to it?" she said. "The desert?"

"On the Internet."

"Then how do you know you'd like it?"

"It's a theory I suspect will prove true."

"Boy wants to get away, huh? From what?" She knocked her knee against mine.

"You've been?" I said. "To the desert?"

"My father's friend owns a preserve in the heart of the Great Basin."

"Whose doesn't? The Great Basin being in New Mexico, of course."

"Utah, Lawrence. It overlaps Nevada too, and Oregon, Idaho, Wyoming, California."

"But not New Mexico, Drikipedia? Not even a little bit?"

"Not even for you."

"Poor me."

"Poor New Mexico," she said. "We spent a Christmas week out there in Utah. It was beautiful. Beyond beautiful." She double squeezed my hand. "But, you know, as stunning as it was out there, it was too lonely for me. Stef's not going to make it, is she?"

"We'll cross paths with somebody."

“The way you say it, I want to believe you.” She touched my left side and rested her hand on my rib cage, midway down the line of the surgery scar. “Can I ask you again?” she said.

“You just did,” I said.

“It looks like it hurts.”

“It was a long time ago,” I said.

“But it still hurts.” She rested her hand on my heart.

Stef whispered in Portuguese. She was watching us.

“What was that, sweetheart?” Dri said. “You’re thirsty, I know.” She put her ear to Stef’s mouth. Stef gulped and cleared her throat and whispered again.

I checked the water distiller. “We have maybe a mouthful for her,” I said.

Dri shook her head no. “She doesn’t want any,” Dri said. “She said she saw them yesterday. Your scars. She said they’re bullet wounds.”

Hearing the words, I felt the dull heat that pulsed whenever somebody made me remember. The heat radiated outward from where the bullet went in just below my left shoulder blade. I shrugged. “I was in the wrong place at the wrong time,” I said. I saw she wanted me to tell her more, but I couldn’t, not with John in earshot. His eyes were dead set on the horizon. JoJo’s too, but I don’t think he was looking out into the ocean as much as looking away from what was happening to Stef. She was turning pale except for under her eyes where the skin was purple.

Dri was kneeling next to Stef but still an arm's reach from me. She took my hand, and her fingers stitched the spaces between mine. She spoke quietly. "You can tell me about it, you know?"

I knew I could, even then, after knowing her for only a day. The way she held my hand, the way she looked at me so openly. She was the kind of person you could tell your secrets and know she would keep them, but I gave her what John always gave me whenever we dared to let it—that night—creep up on us. "It's just what happened," I said.

"I don't mean to push you," she said. She had more to say, but I cut her off.

"I appreciate that," I said. I closed my eyes and rested the back of my head against the side of the boat. It felt like a betrayal to Mr. Costello, talking about the shooting with anybody except John or maybe my dad. He was there too.

I'm still trying to understand what happened that rainy night not long after I turned fourteen. I know this much: It didn't end that night. Three years later, it had followed us onto the water, and now we were trapped with it. Payments were going to have to be made, favors returned, accounts reckoned, sacrifices honored, all the things John and I had managed to dodge until now.

# 12

*Thursday, August 19, just after midnight, the beginning of the second day on the water . . .*

We were too tired to keep two people on watch. We kept nodding off. The waves had gone from making us seasick to rocking us to sleep. Better to have one wide-awake person on lookout while the other three rested up. I took the midnight to three shift. I checked on Stef. Her arm was dead, black from the tourniquet down with a faint scent of rot, but she seemed the most peaceful yet. She'd stopped shivering and her breathing came easier as she slept. These were not good signs.

No boats passed during the three hours of my watch, or I didn't see any lights on the water. I did see some in the sky. They came rhythmically, every couple of minutes. We'd drifted into a flight path. The jets flew too high for their engine noise to reach us.

Toward the end of my shift, JoJo kept me company. I pointed out an even more useless light, a satellite. It moved slowly, a shooting star that didn't want to die.

"You see Lyra behind it, of course," he said.

"Of course."

"You don't like astronomy?"

"I think I'd love it, if I had the time."

"I miss my telescope. When we get back, I must have you down to Rio. Matt, I'm so grateful you're here. You and John. I believe God sent you both. You especially. You revived her. Why do you shake your head? Yes, Matt, you have to accept this truth. You brought Stef back from death."

"She would have coughed up the water anyway, sooner or later."

"I think not. She was drowning. I wouldn't have known what to do. I would have frozen. I did freeze. I never thought I was this kind of person, that I would falter in an emergency situation. I always imagined myself as someone who would be capable in a crisis."

"You were great," I said. "If my girlfriend was in trouble, I would have lost it."

"No. You have a talent for remaining calm. This is the way God made you."

"Inside I was freaking out. I still am."

"But the trick is not to show it, yes? Not in the moment anyway, or else we all would have panicked. Well, maybe not John. He is stonelike in his stillness at times. I mean this as a compliment.

Perfectly steady, your friend. If the nuclear bombs fall, I want to be standing next to John. He will know exactly where to go and what to do, yes?"

"I think he would stay put and crack a Sprite," I said.

"I could see him doing this. He would lie back and put his hands behind his head and say, 'What's next? I'm ready.' Or is John not a believer?"

I didn't know the answer to that. We never talked about stuff like whether or not there was a next life. I guess our minds were tapped out trying to figure out this one. Before I could say anything, JoJo said, "He's a believer. He believes in himself. Matt, who shot you?"

The question woke me up. It always did, but especially now, coming the way it had, from nowhere, or at least not in any way I could connect it to what we'd been talking about, life after death, heaven, hell—there it was, the connection, hell.

"I never found out," I said.

"He got away?"

I checked to see if John was sleeping, and he was. Dri too, and Stef.

"He got away," I said.

"A random act of violence," JoJo said. "I think this would be harder to bear than a deliberate act."

He was so wrong. It was a deliberate act, and it was harder to bear because I was the one who had provoked it. I tried not to see it happening all over again. The more I tried to push it away, the harder it pushed back at me, into my consciousness. I didn't want to blink. In the tenth of a second that my eyes were closed, I would see it, the explosion of car-window glass.

I fiddled with the tiller handle, looking for a way to end the conversation. "What are the chances it'll start when we need it to?" I said.

JoJo patted the boat's engine like it was good dog. "We have a chance now," he said. "We're all going to be okay. I feel it, you know? The morning will come and we'll see a boat. It will be close enough for us to chase it. God is watching out for us. Matt, how about you? Do you believe?"

"Only when I'm taking a test I didn't study for," I said.

"Then you believe." He mussed my hair.

I tried to find a form in the constellation of stars JoJo had pointed out. "So what's Lyra's story?" I said.

"It's an eagle. She's carrying a lyre up to heaven. See?"

"Honestly? No."

He smiled and squinted at the stars. "I don't either. This is why the stars are awesome. You can draw whatever you need into them."

"And why would the ancient Greeks or Romans or whoever need an eagle to fly a lyre up to heaven?"

"Why, so the angels can jam, of course. They knew they were headed that way too, and who doesn't like a good party?"

John stepped toward us. I hadn't noticed when he'd woken up. He took the binoculars from me and said, "Get some sleep."

"You're not on duty for another half hour, boss," JoJo said.

"I'm awake. You guys rest up. I'll wake you at six. And don't call me boss."

"Is that an order?" JoJo said. Now he mussed John's hair. John looked at him like, Why are you touching my hair?

JoJo lay next to Stef. I lay next to Dri. There was no other place to go. Her head rolled slightly with the waves. She cuddled into me. The boat almost rocked me to sleep. When I closed my eyes I saw my parents. Mom paced. Dad kept telling her the same lie I kept telling Dri, that everything was going to be okay.

# 13

**To:** Lieutenant.Stacy.Quintana@suffolkcountypolice.gov

**From:** Detective.Mark.Kreizler@suffolkcountypolice.gov

**Subject:** Update on Missing Persons Costello/Halloway

**Date:** August 19, 4:50 AM

The friend whose car they borrowed says Halloway is a stand-up guy but he wasn't so sure about Costello. I ran background checks, and Halloway looks clean so far. Costello has a weapons possession charge. It was dismissed. I know a guy in Queens County Court who's going to look into it for me. For now, I'm thinking this is just a joyride that got out of hand.

Also, Costello's mother was hospitalized with alcohol poisoning. Apparently this wasn't the first time.

# 14

*August 19, dawn of the second day . . .*

Another sailor joined us that morning. I met him in my nightmare. He lay in the front seat of the car with his skull smashed in. Mr. Costello opened his eyes and cried blood tears. The ghost had never spoken to me before, but that morning he said, *Matt, it's time to wake up.*

I woke up to fog. Dri held my hand in her sleep. I thought someone had put a wood chip into my mouth, until I realized it was my tongue. Now I was the one wondering if I could have just a sip of seawater. Somehow I still had to pee. I slipped away from Driana.

The fog was thick and drizzly, and I couldn't see much past the edge of the boat. John stood at the bow, his arms folded across his chest. He nodded Stef's way.

She died with her eyes and mouth open. That beautiful young woman who was joking around less than a day and a half earlier was just nowhere. I'd seen bodies in caskets, but I'd seen a body like this—raw, ugly dead—only once before. I must have been staring at her, what had been her, for a minute before I realized the drizzle had turned to rain. It fell so hard the fiberglass rang. The ringing woke Dri and JoJo. Dri was midstretch when she noticed Stef. "Why are her eyes open? Why is her mouth open?"

Dri looked like she'd been in a car crash, just dazed, sitting there in the middle of the wreckage, but JoJo was flipping out. He shook Stef's body. He broke the strips of towel that kept the body tied to the windsurf board. He ripped away the sail that mummified her. He grabbed Stef's head in his gigantic hands and brought it to his face and screamed at her in Portuguese, as if yelling could wake her up, could make her face not be paler than the fog. Like shaking her could stop her body from being limp the way a body is when it has no muscle tone. He tried to revive her, mouth to mouth, the way I had two nights before. He was a quick study, because the air went into her lungs no problem. Her chest expanded unnaturally, too quickly, and collapsed just as unnaturally as JoJo hyperventilated her. I tried to make him stop. When Dri snapped out of her daze enough to help me, we were able to pull him off Stef.

The last breath he'd gotten into her body made an awful sound as it came out, screeching train brakes.

John got in there and pulled the tarp off Stef.

"John, hey, wait," Dri said. "*Stop.*"

"What are you doing, man?" I said. I had been trying to cover the body with the tarp when John yanked it away.

"Catching the water," John said. "Matt, wake up. A little help here?"

I left Dri's side and stretched out the tarp with John. We funneled the rain into the milk crate Dri had lined with the plastic tarp. It would hold maybe a cubic foot of water, which seemed like a lot at that moment. JoJo covered Stef's face with his hands. "Help me, Driana," he said. "The rain is getting into her eyes. Help me close her eyes. It's getting into her mouth. She's going to choke."

"JoJo," Dri said.

He cut her off. "Just help me, will you? Help me keep her eyelids *down*. Why won't they stay closed?"

The rain smashed the tops of our heads. Before long the milk crate was full. John dunked the gallon jug into it. He pushed the jug into Dri's hands. "Drink," he said. "Drink all you can, both of you, before the rain stops."

"She was a sister to me, John," Dri said.

"That's all the more reason for you to hurry up and drink."

"Are you kidding? The last thing on my mind right now is *water*."

"Do what you want," John said. "Drink or end up like her." He dunked the peanut can into the milk crate and drank. I cupped water in my hands and drank until my stomach stretched.

By noon the rain was long gone and the sun was the hottest I'd felt it all summer. The water was flat. No breeze, no birds, no fish.

JoJo cradled Stef's body. He was almost as pale as the corpse. He whispered to it. I'd managed to close the eyes after holding them down for a few minutes, and I'd pulled up the Windsurfer sail over the face, but JoJo slipped it down. The eyes didn't stay closed for long either. The heat was working its nasty magic, and the inside of the body was beginning to swell even as the skin was drying out and shrinking. The eyelids pulled back, and the eyes were starting to look like cheese mold. Dri looked away, out at the sea. Where else could she look?

I hadn't needed much time at all to become emotionally distant about Stef's death. Almost right away I'd stopped thinking of the corpse as *her* and started referring to it as, well, *it* in my mind anyway. How had I been able to make this switch so quickly? My coldness frightened me. My John-like practicality. Still, I didn't dare to suggest that maybe we wanted to get the corpse out of the boat before the skin split. The sun was cruel enough that day to bloat the body quickly. Then a more horrific thought came to me: The sun wasn't being cruel at all. It was just being what it was, a mindless, merciless star that would shine on whatever got in its way, beauty or horror, without prejudice, with equal heat. It was everywhere I looked, in the fabric of the water, the sky, the rare wind gust: no spirit, no feeling, emptiness.

We'd put the water in the bench cabinet to keep it as cool as we could. The gallon jug and milk crate were full. "We should limit ourselves to a gallon a day," John said.

"That gets us through tomorrow," I said, "and then we're back to relying on the distiller Dri put together."

"A gallon for all of us, a quart each," John said. "That'll see us through the next four days or so."

"You really think we'll be out here that long?" Dri said.

"Does it matter what I think?"

"We have to run into somebody at some point," I said.

"Why?" John said. "Nobody owes us anything."

"Save your strength, John," Dri said. "Don't let it burn you out. I'm talking about your anger."

"I'm not angry," John said. "I was stating a fact, that we got ourselves out here, and we're the ones who have the biggest incentive to get ourselves back to land. Relying on magical thinking, like we're blessed or whatever, isn't going to save us. It's going to kill us. We're not special. All you have to do is look at your cousin's body to know that. For all her money, she . . . Look, if anything, I'm a little scared."

"Yeah, huh?" Dri said. "You don't look the least bit scared, and maybe that's the most frightening thing of all."

"You'll believe me or you won't. I have no control over that, but there's no anger here. Anger will get me killed faster than anything else, and I'm not ready to give up just yet."

"Oh, you're angry all right," Dri said. "You just don't realize it. And I agree with you on one thing at least. Anger can only get us killed, especially out here. Your best bet is to forgive Stef. Not for her. I know you don't believe in ghosts or whatever."

"Okay, if you say so," John said.

"For you, I'm saying. Forgive her for your own peace of mind."

"I'm sorry about Stef," John said. "I feel bad for you, for him too." He nodded at JoJo, but JoJo wasn't listening. He was cradling the corpse. The body looked smaller in his giant arms. "Seriously," John said, "the last thing I can afford right now is to waste time being mad at Stef."

"Then you better figure out what's making you mad, before it's too late," Dri said.

John didn't look angry, though, and he didn't need to get in the last word either. He shrugged and took up his lookout post at the back of the boat.

I brought Dri a tin of water.

"Are you hungry?" she said.

"You're not?" I said. The last thing I'd eaten was that mouthful of turkey at Dri's party, close to forty hours before.

"I was famished yesterday," she said, "but today not so much. Does that mean I'm losing it?" She looked over the bow, into the water close to the boat. "I used to think the ocean teemed with fish, but it's like the land. Everybody wants to live in the prime spots, and the rest is desert."

"What did they tell you in your survival class about how long a person can go without food?" I said.

"A long time."

"That's what I thought."

"What do I tell my uncle? When we get back, I mean. Do I tell him Stef killed herself doing something insane? Or was it insanely beautiful? Flying like that at midnight. The moon, the stars. She died like she lived. She lived like she could die at any moment. She didn't squander life. She revered it. She was the one who got me interested in being a vet in the first place. She was always taking in stray dogs, feeding cats in the parks. If she found a sick pigeon in the street, she'd take it home and nurse it back to health, and if it died she'd be weepy for days. She was a year older, but that's a big deal when you're a kid. She was my hero.

"I think you would have liked her a lot. I think John would have too. If she said she felt connected to him, she was. Stef was rarely wrong about people. She came across as stuck-up at first, I know, but that was just her insecurity. Once you got to know her a little and she felt she could trust you, she would let you see who she really was, who she always would've been, that sad little girl who worried over the street doves."

"Stef was right," I said.

"About what, and why are you whispering?"

"I need to cool off. We both do." We slipped into the water on the shady side of the boat and stayed low in it, our mouths just above the surface.

"Stef was right about John," I said. "About the kinship she wanted to feel with him. It's hard to talk about this with anybody except John, and even that's almost impossible, but I want to tell you about the shooting."

# 15

*August 19, afternoon . . .*

The water was cool and then cooler when Dri traced the starburst scar on my left shoulder blade with her fingertip. "That's where it went in, the bullet?" she said. "Where did it come out?"

"It didn't," I said, "and that was the problem." We kept our voices low and our heads above water by holding on to the side of the boat. With our free hands we gripped each other's fingers like we'd known each other a lot longer than two days. Fear brings people together fast. I felt in every part of me, humming and whirring at the atomic level, that she was changing me. If it—if *we*—didn't work out I wouldn't be able to go back to being who I was. She had opened up to me, had let me into her beautiful, shiny life, into Stef's tortured one, and now it was my turn.

"It was a .22 caliber bullet," I said. "A .22 tumbles around when it hits you. The surgeons had to go hunting for it. I was on the table for six hours. They found it in my hip. That was after it went through my left lung."

"But you're okay now?" she said. "That was a stupid question. Of course you can't be okay after something like that."

"When it's humid and I'm running or whatever, my rib cage aches where the bullet cracked it. Other than that I'm okay."

"I meant okay in your heart," she said. "How did it happen?"

I had to grit my teeth for a second to keep them from chattering. We'd drifted into an even colder patch of water. "It was messed up. John and I were fourteen."

"Wait, John was there?"

"We were in the backseat of Mr. Costello's Honda. John's dad's car, the minivan he used for work. His tools were piled around us: electric cables, a portable generator. Mr. Costello was driving. My dad was there too, in the shotgun seat. We were on our way home from a night game. Baseball, summer league. We would have lost if the rain hadn't washed us out. My dad kept turning around to look at us. He was nodding and smiling, and so was Mr. Costello. I remember the fast food signs lit their faces red, grimy yellow. Mr. Costello said what we had done was beautiful, perfect. We were true champions or whatever."

"What, you guys never gave up, even though you were losing like that?" Dri said.

"There was this guy getting picked on, in the bleachers. He was the assistant coach on the other team, and he had Down syndrome. He managed the equipment. He remembered everybody's name, cheered for both sides, had a nice word for everybody. These idiots show up in the stands, and they start giving the guy a hard time, calling him retard, chucking pebbles at the back of his head, snapping at his ears or whatever when he isn't looking."

"That kind of thing makes me furious enough to where I think I could actually kill someone," Dri said.

"Toward the end of the game the leader of this crew of knuckleheads spits on the back of the assistant coach's neck. We stop play right there, all of us, and we say we won't start until the idiots leave the ballpark. Now the umpires are getting into it, and the parents, and everybody's screaming at these psychos that they better get out of there, or do they want the cops to come and make them leave? So they go, but not before they curse everybody out and knock over the water cooler, whip ice at everybody, and there's shoving and threats and whatever."

"Geniuses," Dri said.

"Okay, so they're out of there, and a little later the rain ends the game, and we're on our way home. The rain is ridiculous. A pond's growing in the middle of Woodhull Road, the main drag where John and I come from. The elevated train's rumbling overhead. The tracks separate Brooklyn and Queens. Right there on the borderline I'm about to become somebody else, somebody I'm not ready to be."

"Who's this person you think you became?"

"Somebody who . . . I don't know. Who feels safer when he's alone, maybe?"

"Matthew, no. You're not meant to be alone—especially you."

"We stopped at a red light. I'm oiling my catcher's mitt to avoid looking into our fathers' eyes, their smiles. 'Pizza or burgers?' Mr. Costello says, and that's the last thing he says. A white SUV pulls alongside."

"The idiots from the bleachers."

"Mr. Costello's window sprays in on us. His neck sprays out. It's happening all at once, you know? The train brakes are screeching, the pigeons are scattering, my face is burning. I can't tell whose blood is in my mouth, Mr. Costello's or mine. The windshield wipers keep going, tick-tock, tick-tock. The car's still in gear, and the van's creeping forward. The backseat window glass blows in, and I see the shooter, the gun in the dude's hand, the grin. His arm comes down like a falling tree. The gun points into the backseat and levels out. He's walking alongside the car, lining up his shot."

"God, you're shivering."

The boat had gradually turned around in the water, and now we were hunkering on its sunlit side, but even the sun burned cold. "It wasn't the blood that freaked me out. It was that the wind was knocked out of me, completely, like I'd been tackled by a linebacker, no pads, no helmet. I was dizzy from the whiplash. I'm trying to gulp that first breath when I see the car isn't creeping forward anymore. It's peeling out."

"The shooter's car?"

"No, the one we're trapped in, Mr. Costello's van, except my dad is behind the wheel now."

"He didn't get hit?" Dri said.

"Mr. Costello took all three bullets fired into the front seat. His body is pinned against the driver's side door. My dad's hammering the gas, because they're still shooting at us. We don't get too far though. A tire blows out and the minivan coasts into one of the iron columns that hold up the train tracks. You know what? I'm sorry I'm telling you this all of a sudden, especially now."

"Matthew, now is the only time, the best time. Keep going."

"I'm walking away from where the car hit the train trestle. My dad's following me. He's covered in like this pinkish airbag dust. Freaky. He's got a whip mark across the side of his neck from where a cable hit him when Mr. Costello's tools went flying. Dad keeps telling me to sit my butt down on the curb there, but I'm pushing him away. I just have to walk it off and catch my breath, I keep telling him. Just leave me alone. Then these EMTs are trying to strap me down to a backboard. I can't get them to understand it's not my spine that hurts, it's my chest. I'm a little winded, get your hands off me, right? I mean, I'm swinging at these guys."

"I totally get it. Everybody's trying to hold you down."

"Except for the lead EMT. She's calm, so calm. She tells everybody to give me some room, and they do. 'Hiya there, Matt,' she says. Her voice is soft but deep, and she's in no rush to get the words out. She asks me if I remember what happened. I tell her somebody tried to shoot me, but I'm okay, I'm just a little short of breath. She says, 'Let's try to make that better then. Let's breathe together, slowly, deeply.' So I breathe. She has these beautiful tattoos. They're hieroglyphs. They start at her fingertips and go all the way up her forearms and maybe higher, because I see the tips of them peeking out over her shirt collar. She's a big woman, in her fifties. The way she's standing there so at ease, you just know she's been doing this a long time."

"She sounds amazing."

"My dad's yelling at me to do what the lady says, and she puts a soft hand on Dad's shoulder and says, 'It's okay. Matt's okay. I got this,' and my dad chills right out."

"Where's John in this?"

"He's there. Right there. He's solid."

"All those tools flying around when the car crashed, and he didn't get hurt?"

"I know," I said. "It was otherworldly," and it was. "The way this lead EMT is talking to me, so calmly, I just do whatever she says. I lie back and let them tie me up to the board, and I breathe with her. I quiet down inside. It feels good to be told what to do by somebody who so clearly knows what she's doing. An oxygen mask goes over my mouth and nose, and now I'm on a stretcher, and they're wheeling me toward the ambulance. My dad is shaking like its twenty degrees out, not ninety."

"And John?" Dri said. "Is he shaking?"

"He's a rock."

"Of course."

"He's walking next to the stretcher. His hand's on my shoulder. 'You're okay, Matt,' he tells me, and the way he says it, I believe him. I ask him where his dad is, and he says, 'Don't worry about that now, breathe easy,' like the EMT told me to do. I have to know though. 'Just tell me,' I say. 'Did he make it?' And John says, 'No, now stop talking and breathe, like she said.' I follow his eyes. He's tracking her, the lead EMT. 'Man, she's good,' John says. 'She moves like she's walking underwater.'

Dri squeezed my hand. "You're shaking all over," she said.

"I woke up two days later in the hospital, and I felt like . . . You ever hit your finger with a hammer? I'm ringing hot all over my body, but that's nothing compared to how busted up I am about the fact that these maniacs are going to get away with killing Mr. Costello, that they're still out there. That they'll always be out there. My dad was able to grab a shaky shot of the SUV's license plate, but the car turned out to be stolen. They'd planned it perfectly, how to hit us and get away clean, and I was a total idiot not to see it coming."

"Matthew, there's absolutely no way you could have known they would take it that far. I want you to listen to me now. It wasn't your fault. They didn't single you out. It was random. What happened could have happened to anybody else at the ballpark. Those guys were going to kill somebody that night; who didn't matter. They just happened to pick John's dad's van to follow. You need to understand that."

A horsefly buzzed by Dri and landed on my lip. It snapped me out of the memory of that night three years in the past but so not gone, so here with us in the water.

"You can tell me, okay?" she said.

"Tell you what?"

"The rest of the story. I won't push you. Whenever you're ready, you tell me what you need to say."

How she knew there was more is just proof that she was from someplace else, someplace better, a world to come maybe, where people just know. Here her cousin died, and she's worried about me. I might have told her the rest of it right then, the parts I left out, even the worst part, if I hadn't noticed John's shadow on the water. He was looking down at us. "I think you two need to see this," he said.

I pulled myself up over the side of the boat. JoJo slapped the corpse's face. That was the start of them, the flies.

# 16

**To:** Lieutenant.Stacy.Quintana@suffolkcountypolice.gov

**From:** Detective.Mark.Kreizler@suffolkcountypolice.gov

**Subject:** Update on Missing Persons Costello/Halloway

**Date:** Friday, August 20, 10:53 AM—Day 3

The car turned up on Dune Road, home of Rafael Gonzaga. I got the transcript for the hearing related to the weapons charge on Costello. It was for a sawed-off pipe found in his backpack. He was fourteen at the time. He told the judge he was worried that the people who killed his father would try to get him too, if they saw him out on the street. The judge asked John if he thought he would be able to do it, to hit somebody in the head with a club. John said, "Definitely." There's a note in the transcription that John didn't hesitate when he said that. The judge said, "Good for you, for telling the truth, but leave the pipe at home next time." The charge was dropped.

# 17

*Saturday, August 21, just after midnight and the beginning of the fourth day on the water . . .*

The sky was too clear and the moon too bright. The body didn't look anything like Stef now. It didn't look human anymore either. It had swelled even more quickly than I thought it would. Its—her face had split at a laugh line. We'd wrapped her in the windsurfing sail to keep the flies off her, but they kept coming anyway, more and more of them. The sail seemed less a shield to them and more of a fast food billboard, stained brown with her blood and yellow with her plasma where the blood chips flaked away.

"Maybe there's a ship nearby?" JoJo said. "A freighter transporting livestock?"

Nobody bothered to answer him. We hadn't seen any boats for more than a day.

“Maybe they hitched a ride on a fishing boat,” JoJo said. He’d been going on like this since the day before, throwing out one theory after another about how horseflies could end up in the middle of the ocean. “The boat dumped a rotten carcass or a spoiled haul, right? The flies piggybacked on the dead fish until they picked up Stef’s scent.”

“God, Jo, stop talking about it,” Dri said. “Please, okay? How they got here doesn’t matter. They’re here.” We all were on edge, even John a little, after more than three days without food.

“I’m just saying maybe there’s a boat around, Dri,” JoJo said. Then he spoke to Stef’s corpse in Portuguese. He turned to John and said, “I was telling her that maybe there’s a boat around.”

John looked away from JoJo. I’d say it was a gesture of contempt, except his face was blank.

The flies were fast, uncatchable. They got under our clothes. If you’ve ever held a lit match too long, that’s a horsefly bite. The pain is almost unnoticeable at first, and then second by second the heat doubles and deepens until you want to claw the burning out of your skin. JoJo got the worst of them because he refused to leave Stef’s side. His face and arms were raw where he scratched his welts. A fly landed on Stef’s broken lip. JoJo shooed it and cursed God.

“There’s only one way to get rid of them,” John said.

“John, I know, okay?” Dri said.

“We have to give them what they want.”

“I get it,” Dri said. “Just . . .”

"What?"

"Never mind," she said.

"Okay," John said.

"I was going to say just relax, but you're sitting there like a vampire anyway."

"A vampire. Great."

"You're too *still.* God."

"Still. I can totally see why that would be a problem for you. Shall I dance for you, princess?"

"You can't be nice, can you?" Dri said. "That's a serious question, John. You know what? Don't bother to answer. I feel bad for you."

"You don't need to, really," he said. "In fact I'd prefer you didn't."

"But I do. Just when I really want to like you, you remind me of why that's so very hard."

"You don't need to like me, Dri. You just need to finish this ride with me, and then we'll never see each other again. Don't sweat yourself on my account."

"I do need to like you, though. You need to be liked, and it makes me so sad that you just don't know this. I'm sorry for you, John. Truly I am. I can't imagine what it would be like, my dad being killed right in front of me."

John had no reaction to that. "The body," he said. "We have to make a decision here. Matt, any chance at all you're going to weigh in?"

"You don't have to put him in the middle," Dri said.

"I don't want him in the middle," John said. "I need him on my side."

As it turned out I happened to be sitting between them. Yes, the flies were chewing at me as much as they were John, and yes, I agreed with what he was thinking, but no, I wasn't going to tell Dri we had to dump her cousin's body. I'd told her too much already, spilling the grimy details of the Woodhull Road mess. I regretted it now, my need to *share* or whatever, to infect her with the sense of loss that took hold of me under the train tracks that night and never let me go, as if talking about it would halve the pain instead of double it.

I cupped my hand and swung harder than I had to at a fly chewing my shoulder through my shirt. I was shaky with a hunger pang. The cramp went almost as quickly as it came, and I didn't feel any better, just weaker.

"JoJo," Dri said. "Look at me, sweetie. It's time."

"Your uncle will die if he doesn't get to say good-bye to her," JoJo said. A fly landed on his lip now. He could have swatted it away, but instead he smacked himself.

"He can't say good-bye, Jo," Dri said. "She's gone. Look at her. It's killing me. We have to let her go."

"How can you not see that I have to bring her home to Rio?" JoJo said. "She has to go into the crypt. This is her destiny. Did you know that your uncle had a crypt made for Stef's mother?"

We all did. He'd told us about it twice already. "I know, Jo," Dri said.

JoJo cut her off. "I used to go with Stef," he said. "These huge pine trees shade the crypt. She'll be happy there. She'll be with her mom. You understand, don't you? This way I can visit her. Please, I am begging you, Dri. Matt, you see where I am coming from, right?"

"I do, JoJo." I had more to say, starting off with "but," until JoJo cut me off.

"Thank you, Matt. She thanks you too." He brought Stef's face to his chest to shield it from the flies. "Yes, *meu amor*. I'm taking you home."

John slung his arm over my shoulder. "Nice job, bud. Your pal Dri there was a breath away from getting crazy man to give up the corpse. You're the smartest guy I know, but you don't know when to speak up and when to shut up. When will you ever learn, man?" He grabbed at a fly on my arm and actually caught it. He crushed it, and another took its place.

For the next few hours, Dri begged JoJo to let go of Stef's body. She hugged him; she hugged Stef's corpse. She stroked his hair and hers. She cried, laughed, and remembered with him. All the while the flies gnawed on us. The biting got so bad I had to slip into the water and stay there for a bit, much as I hated being in the ocean in the dark. Finally, at sunrise, Dri convinced JoJo to give up Stef.

We took back the sail, the strips of towel, even the tourniquet crusty with blood. Stef wore a silver choker. A medal hung from it, the dove of peace. I unclipped the necklace and gave it to Dri.

"No, leave it on her," Dri said.

"No, Dri, you take it," JoJo said.

We put the body on the windsurf board. JoJo said some prayers in Portuguese and we laid the board in the water. The ocean was flat then, but when the waves came the body would wash off the board. We only needed it to stay above water until we paddled away.

John and I paddled while Dri and JoJo watched the body grow smaller. I kept my eyes steady ahead until we were a hundred yards off, and then I looked back. The body's grisliness wasn't obvious anymore. JoJo took out his phone. "Matt, can you turn the boat a little right? I want to line up a picture of my angel with the sun in the background. Yes, that's it. This will be my last memory of her, forever part of the sunrise." *Click.*

Stef took the flies with her. Not all of them, and not all at once, but in a few minutes only a few ragged stragglers remained. They were easy kills.

# 18

**To:** Lieutenant.Stacy.Quintana@suffolkcountypolice.gov

**From:** Detective.Mark.Kreizler@suffolkcountypolice.gov

**Subject:** Costello/Halloway

**Date:** Saturday, August 21, 12:50 PM—Day 4

MISSING PERSONS SUFFOLK COUNTY 314-0818 COSTELLO/HALLOWAY ***EXPANDED***

Also presumed missing:
Gonzaga, Driana, 17, of Manhattan
Gonzaga, Estefania, 18, of Rio de Janeiro
Martins, João, 18, of Rio de Janeiro

Driana Gonzaga appears to be universally loved. The locals are starting up a search party for her. We checked her friends' Instagrams and found a shot of her and Matt Halloway holding hands on the beach the night of the party. That's where the search focus is for now, on the cliffs and dunes. Lots of places to hide bodies, neighbors say, but I don't buy it. Everything I'm getting on Halloway from his coworkers and teachers is he's the perfect kid, nice, quiet—very quiet. He doesn't even have a Facebook page, no Instagram, no social media whatsoever. Costello doesn't either, but I'm less sure about him. One of his coworkers referred to him as the Iceman.

# 19

*Sunday, August 22, morning, day five . . .*

Our water supply was starting to look scary, and what little we dared to drink we sweated right out. The dehydration cramped my legs so bad my hamstrings twitched. I tried to rub the knots out of the muscles but that only exhausted me. My circulatory system was getting messed up too, because even though it was a hundred-plus degrees in that boat my feet were cold. Meanwhile my head and shoulders were on fire. John had made a turban from his T-shirt and kept the turban wet. Blisters speckled his shoulders.

"Better put your shirt on," I said.

"I'd rather keep my head cool," he said.

Time slowed down sometimes and sped up others. The morning passed in a blink, and then the sun stalled at noon. "Move," I said. "Get going. Go down." My voice sounded strange to me, how

I might sound as an old man, if I lived long enough. Most of the day before, my stomach felt punched in, but today I wasn't hungry at all, like I was just getting over the flu. I was too tired to sleep but too drowsy to be awake, too sick to dream. I guess that was a good thing. I wasn't coughing as much as I had been the first couple of days. That had been rough, getting used to breathing in the saltwater air. Still, my lungs itched deep down.

Now that Stef and the flies were gone, the sense of urgency had left the boat. We seemed to move in slow motion. My arms were heavy when I put the binoculars to my eyes. The binoculars probably weighed a pound but felt twenty times that. When I was alone on watch and Dri was asleep—that was the worst time. The real drag about being stuck on the water is the monotony. Even the constant feeling of terror becomes boring. And after the first few hours of being amazed by the sea's wideness and the clouds that look like angels one minute and trolls the next, there's nothing to look at, no place to go but inward, and who wants to go there, especially when a ghost is waiting for you?

The one thing we had plenty of was wind. We tried all kinds of ways to rig up the Windsurfer sail. It was stained with orangey reminders of Stef's suffering. We tied the mast to the railings that ran along the front of the boat with a complicated web of towrope. The sail caught the wind until the mast creaked against the towrope and fell. We applied more rope. The sail held the wind and stayed up and almost flipped the boat. We lowered the sail, the flag of our incompetence. Even if we'd figured out a way to make it work, we wouldn't have known which way to sail. We were able to figure out north, south, east, and west with John's wristwatch, but we didn't know which one of those would take us to land. We could have been twenty miles off the Brooklyn coast for all we knew, or twenty from Boston, or two hundred from nowhere. Everywhere I looked, looked exactly the same.

Then at about two in the afternoon we finally saw a bird, a gull. Not long after that we saw fish, very small and silver. They followed along in the boat's shadow. We tried to catch them with our hands, but they were too fast or we were too slow.

JoJo spoke to me in Portuguese.

"My brain isn't working well enough to try to translate that," I said.

"Maybe big fish will come to eat the small ones," he said. His smile sagged, his face darkened. The light went out of his eyes, and they turned muddy indigo. He drew his phone and shot a video of himself. He spoke in Portuguese.

Dri hugged him. "Stop talking like that, Jo. Your mom already knows you're grateful to her." She turned to me. "He said he's grateful to his mom for having him." Back to JoJo: "You're going to tell her that yourself, Jo, in person. You'll see her again very soon, sweetheart. You just watch."

Dri's hug cheered him up. It cheered me up too. Our feelings were so transferable out there. Being together with nowhere to run, we were forced to absorb one another's moods. Well, three of us were. Only John was immune to our fears and hopes. JoJo was John's opposite. More than Dri and me, he picked up on any little shift in someone's emotional state and magnified it. With Dri's hand in his, the light was back in his eyes. "Here, come, Matt. Come, John. Today's memory will be a video of the four of us. Lean in."

"We need to save that battery," John said.

"Just for a moment," JoJo said. "When we get home I am going to post all the memories of her, for her family. The story of her last adventure. Humor me, John. Please?"

John was making a harpoon from the Windsurfer's handrail. He scored an end of it with the flat-head screwdriver. "Then you'll turn off the phone?" he said.

"We'll be quick." We huddled, and JoJo framed us. "Dri, tap record. Thank you. Okay, so we are four days on the water, and, well, we are *here*. We will not be defeated. We will carry Stef's memory home. Dri?"

"We have each other."

"That's all?" JoJo said.

"That's everything," she said.

"Yes. Now you, Matt," JoJo said.

Dri was leaning into me. The backs of our hands were touching. I slipped my fingers between hers, and she gripped my hand good. "I'm relieved," I said. In the phone's screen I saw Dri and JoJo smile in confusion. John just looked confused. "I was stuck for what to write about in my college essay," I said.

"John?"

"Five, not four," John said. "We're five days on the water."

At dusk John called me over to help him with the harpoon. "Sit on the bench and hold the pipe steady," he said.

He lined up a hammer with the end of the pipe and swung down. The pipe cracked along the lines he scored into it. I touched the end of the harpoon, and it was sharper than the old kitchen knives we had back home in Queens—not that they were being used much. No way had my parents eaten a thing since I'd gone missing. I couldn't think about it, about them. I had to save my energy, and I wasn't going to burn away my calories on tears.

John wasn't as interested in the harpoon as he was in the short end he'd snapped off.

He wrapped a handle onto it—Stef's plasma-stained tourniquet. "It's a knife," he said.

"I picked up on that," I said.

"To butcher the fish."

"What fish?"

"The one I'm going to catch."

"How?"

"I'm still working on that." He wore the knife in his belt.

... — — — ...

I was alone on lookout duty as the seconds ticked away toward midnight. I watched the date change from *Aug 22* to *Aug 23* on JoJo's phone. *Sun* became *Mon*, and acid burned the lining of my stomach. This was the start of our sixth day on the water. I turned off the phone and stowed it in my pocket. I didn't see anything out there worth a battery-draining SOS flash.

JoJo was supposed to relieve me but I let him sleep. The flies had chewed on all of us equally by now, but JoJo's bites weren't healing. He wouldn't stop digging at them—or couldn't stop, he said. He was as close to peaceful as he was going to get, snoring away in the back of the boat, and I wasn't sleepy anyway. It wasn't the stars that were keeping me awake. Even they couldn't amaze me anymore. It was Dri, the idea that we might hang out together after we were saved, *if* we were saved. I pictured the two of us doing regular stuff, picking out that dog, the one she was going to rescue in September. Meeting up with her at the animal shelter and heading out for a slice or two after. Lying in the grass together at the North Meadow in Central Park, trying to find faces in the clouds. Cuddling up with her on the sofa while we watched corny old movies or great ones, *Lawrence of Arabia* maybe. Isn't that what you do with your girlfriend? I didn't know. I'd never gotten that close with anybody. I'd had crushes, and most of the people I hung out with at school were girls, but it wouldn't be right to start up something serious with one of them. I was friendly with everybody but wouldn't allow myself to have actual friends outside of John. When people tried to get close, I pulled back. I was a loner, and I felt better that way. It's not fair to ask a girl to be with somebody who can't really be with her. But Dri was different. I couldn't see myself *not* being with her. I think it was the sand castle she built with that kid. The one that lasted forever when you remembered it. That was Dri. The world could wash away, and she would still be there with that lopsided smile, the one that made me smile just thinking about it.

Something chirped, John's phone alarm. He woke himself up to turn it off. "What's with the grin?" he said. "Matt, don't start losing it on me." Our self-appointed timekeeper, he nudged JoJo with his foot. "Hey, you're up," he said. "*Jo*Jo."

"Uh?" JoJo rubbed his eyes and seemed not to know where he was.

"You're late for your watch," John said.

JoJo mumbled in Portuguese and then said sorry in English. The giant was woozy, and the boat rocked as he stumbled to his post.

"Matt, sleep," John said.

"I'm fine," I said.

"You need to stick to the schedule. If you don't sleep, you'll fall asleep next time you're on lookout."

We'd stretched the tarp over the front half of the boat to make a sleeping tent. Two people fit under there. We'd made a smaller tent toward the back of the boat with the Windsurfer sail. It was big enough for two people, but we designated that one for Dri whenever she wasn't on watch. It was the better tent. You could see the sky through the sail a little bit, in between Stef's bloodstains anyway, even at night if the moon was high enough. It wasn't so claustrophobic. The tarp the boys slept under was as dark during the day as it was at night, but because it was plastic-coated canvas, it was much warmer than the tent we'd made with the Windsurfer sail. I crawled under the tarp and was almost settled in when I felt Dri's hand on my ankle. I sat up. "You okay?" I said.

"Freezing. Come here."

John was back under the tarp in his sleeping vampire pose, hands folded over his chest, but JoJo was awake enough now to have heard Dri. He looked sad. "Matt, what are you waiting for?" he said. "She's cold. Here, take this too." He gave me his hoodie to give to Dri. She was already wearing one, but it was thin. When he pulled off his hoodie his shirt came up too, and his back was covered with sores. "JoJo," I said, but he cut me off.

"I know. I won't scratch. Now go to Driana."

I crawled under the sail and cuddled Dri. She was shivering. "She's been gone almost four days now," she said, "but each time I wake up I look for her for a few seconds, until I remember this isn't a dream. JoJo was dead-on when he was talking about my uncle Tomás. He's going to lose it. Stef was his world. My dad's too. He loved her like she was his. When we were little we'd get caught doing something stupid, and she would always skate free. I'd get punished for both of us. And—I'm not lying—it was always Stef who got us involved in the mischief in the first place. I guess I didn't have to tell you that. This one time we were in the Ralph Lauren store. I was like eleven. Stef just had to have these sparkly princess hair bands. She stuck one into her pocket, another into mine, and of course she was out the door home free and I got caught. But Stef came back for me. Was she sorry? No. Right in front of the security guard she yelled at me for being such a rotten thief. They made us wait in the security office. I'm a crying mess and Stef's pouting. She made the security guard change the channel on his TV to *Judge Judy*. My dad came and picked us up and didn't say a word until we got home. 'Well, Driana,' he said, 'I'm so disappointed in you I could cry.' Stef was like, 'But, Tio, it was my fault. I was the one who stole them.' And my dad goes, 'No, no, it can't be. Not *my* Estefania. She would never be so naughty.'"

"Which was his way of telling her he was so disappointed in her he could cry," I said.

"Exactly. So maybe she didn't skate. I swear, I know I should be crying, but when I think about her all I want to do is laugh." She was doing a little of both. "My poor dad. This is going to change him. He won't be as hopeful anymore. He struggles with that."

"Hope?"

"I know, he's rich, so the world should be rosy every which way he looks, right? But all the stuff he does with the foundation?

He sees things. He tries to fix one of them, then he takes on two more disasters. Spoiling Stef was one of the great delights in his life."

"How about your mom?" I said.

"What about her?"

"In all the time we've been out here, you haven't mentioned her."

"She moved out. Right after Christmas. I'm still so mad, Matthew. Not about the split. I mean, that part's breaking my heart, but I get it. Things happen—things you couldn't possibly have seen coming—and you change, and you aren't the people you were when you met. It only makes sense at that point to take a break. No, I'm mad because she wanted me to go with her. I just don't know how you ask somebody to do that. I mean, if you have to go, go, but don't ask me to desert my father and leave him with nothing, right? If my dad had left, I would have stayed with my mom. He wouldn't have asked me to go with him, though. He wouldn't have wanted Mom to be alone. But then he never would have left her in the first place. God, I can see her back in her apartment. She's past freaking out by now."

"They all are," I said. "I'm sorry. About your folks."

"They're just separated still. Legally, I mean. She hasn't filed for divorce yet. I'm not pushing them to stay together, just hoping, you know? It's tricky because he has to travel all the time and she's a homebody. Good luck trying to get her to leave New York. Even before they split we could barely get her to come out to East

Hampton. She was thinking about coming out this weekend though, or she promised me she would think about it. She knew my dad was going to be back from London too. I wasn't expecting them to fall into each other's arms all over again, but I was thinking maybe it could be the beginning of a thaw. They'll never get back together now. Not after this."

"I don't know about that," I said. "Tragedy brings people together, right?"

"Not this time. She'll blame him for all of this, beginning with letting me have the party. She says he's too lax with me, and he says she doesn't trust me enough. Sorry, I'll stop there. I could go on all night about the two of them, and thinking about where they are or aren't on fixing themselves only makes me more upset because there's nothing I can do about it out here. There's probably nothing I can do about it back there either. God, I feel like I'm talking at half speed. Am I? It takes a lot longer to find the words. I know I'm starving, but then how come I'm not hungry anymore?"

"We'll run into somebody soon," I said.

"You keep saying that. Thank you."

"For what?"

"What about you?" she said. "Your folks still together? They're cool?"

"They're cool. They're together."

"Nice. Maybe I don't have to worry about you so much after all. Your folks are great, you're at Hudson, you're going to Yale."

"I wish. Been meaning to ask you, can your dad buy them a building for me?"

"You're *going*, okay? So where's this whole desert thing coming from? And by the way, I don't for a minute believe that's going to make you happy. Being alone. Here's my prescription: You and I start hanging out. We have an awesome year next year. I force myself to get over the fact I'm dating a dude who's still in high school. You force yourself to date a girl who cleans animal cages. You with me so far?"

"My second favorite movie is *Rocky.* Ever see it?"

"Am I from Mars? And why are we talking movies all of a sudden?"

"I'm just saying, Rocky's girlfriend, Adrian, she cleaned animal cages."

"And as I recall, Rocky did just fine."

"Well, he lost the fight," I said.

"But he got the girl, so there you go."

"I still can't believe you haven't seen *Lawrence of Arabia.*"

"When we get back, we'll watch it and you'll explain why it's so awesome when the book was only meh. Okay, you finish up at Hudson, next stop Yale. You drop the forestry thing and major in something sensible and incredibly lucrative like film criticism, something that will keep you from running away to the canyons, where they don't have any movie theaters, just so you know. You head on up to Cambridge on the weekends, where I'll be waiting for you at the train station. You study your brains out on that train, okay?"

"Promise."

"You get killer grades, you graduate top of your class, you have your pick of teaching positions."

"Teaching, huh? I don't think so."

"You'll see. Whatever you do, you stay with me in New York, we live happily ever after." She hid her face in my shirt. JoJo turned to see what was up. Then he turned away.

"Why did you have to give me that ice cream?" she said. "Why did you have to get on the boat?"

"I was, I don't know. I was worried about you."

"Oh my God, you just keep making it worse. Why are you doing this to me?"

"What am I doing?"

"Matthew, look at me. What are you running away from?"

John was awake now—and after he'd told me to stick to the sleep schedule too. He'd slipped out from under the tarp and onto the nose of the boat. He was looking into the nearer water.

"We should probably quit while we're ahead," I said. "Or while I'm ahead at least. I had you at happily-ever-after a minute ago. I can only mess this up. We should rest."

Dri kissed my cheek and lay back and rested her head on my chest. She slept, and I didn't sleep a wink. Her hand was resting on my chest too. Her fingers found the gaps in my rib cage. Her fingertips crossed the scar line.

# 20

THE HAMPTONIAN TIMES

## Gonzaga Cousins and João Martins Missing Six Days

BY M. J. SHAW, AUGUST 23, updated 6:32 PM

---

East Hampton—On Main Street, yellow ribbons are appearing everywhere, tied around trees and lampposts with pictures of Driana and Estefania Gonzaga and Mr. Martins. The teens went missing last Tuesday night after a party at Driana Gonzaga's home on Dune Road.

Police won't comment while the investigation is ongoing, but rumors are circulating that authorities aren't ruling out the possibility of a kidnapping. No word has been given as to whether a ransom request has been made. An official close to the investigation reports that detectives are focusing on two young men from Queens, Matthew Halloway and John Costello, both 17.

Mr. Costello's former boss, Michael Garcia of Elite Auto Repair, described Costello as a terrific worker, but "robotic. I always had a funny feeling about John," Garcia said. "He was the kind where you want to put a little distance between yourself and him."

Lifeguards at Heron Hills, where the young men were working this summer, said of Mr. Halloway, "he was too nice sometimes" and "too good to be true."

## Comments (34)

---

**Allison_Sunada**

We love you, Dri. Please come home safe. : . . . ( 👍25

**Coop_15moonwalk**

I heard of Diana Gonazogo from a mutual friend, and she's supposed to be a real good girl. When they catch these losers from Queens, they should string them up. Serious, no mercy. 👍3 👎9

**Gabriela_Azevedo**

Estefa, que o tempo que surfou nas Maldivas foi o melhor momento da minha vida. Eu te amo e JoJo, e eu sei que você vai ficar bem, por favor, Jesus Cristo. 👍1

# 21

*Tuesday, August 24, afternoon, day seven . . .*

"You have to stop scratching," I said. I'd told him plenty of times, and I was getting close to yelling at him.

"Just a few more minutes," JoJo said. "It's the only thing that makes me feel good."

"You're tearing off your skin. Your nails are filthy. You're infecting yourself." I pushed his hand away from his shin. "I mean it, we're going to have to tie your hands behind your back."

"It's not just the fly bites," JoJo said. "My dermatitis flares up when I become stressed. Matt, my medications. I don't do so well when I skip them."

"Just keep washing the sores with salt water and then rinse with the fresh water."

"We don't have enough fresh water. I would rather drink my

share. Anyway, it's not just my skin. I take mood stabilizers, or I did until we rushed out here. So there, we are brothers now, if we weren't already. I let you in on my secret. You're not on medication?"

"I probably should be. Dri says I'm sad."

"Yes, I know. And this tells me that Driana truly does not understand the meaning of the word *sad*."

I didn't like the way he was looking at her. He seemed to be annoyed with her. He had no reason to be. She was asleep under her tent—deeply asleep. Her arms were spread out a little from her sides, her hands palms up. Her head rolled with the waves, leaving her neck exposed. I kept thinking, *Vulnerable. She's so vulnerable.*

It had started the day before, just after sunset. A bad feeling had come into the boat. It wasn't exactly anger. A menace, maybe. I didn't think JoJo was causing it, but he was picking up on it. He took a picture of a sore on the inside of his shin. It looked like raw chicken. He'd lost the most weight. He had the most to lose, and now his jeans hung loose. Mine did too. John was lean to begin with, but his cheekbones were becoming sharper. Dri seemed to be in the best shape, at least up until that point.

I lifted the water jug from the sea. We kept it there with a tow-rope to cool it and slow the bacteria from turning it bad. We'd cut the rations to stretch the supply, but that rainstorm was five long days in the past, and now we were down to a third of a jug. Our ration for today was three sips each. I took one of mine. The water still tasted of gasoline but I had a hard time not chugging it. JoJo held out his hand for the jug. He took all three sips at once. And then he took a fourth.

"Hey," John said.

"What?" JoJo said.

"Easy. You pulled one too many out of the jug."

JoJo cursed. "Sorry. I forgot."

"You're done until we cook up some more," John said, but more was not on the way. Dri's improvised distiller filled two peanut cans a day, and the sky had to be cloudless.

JoJo handed John the jug and curled into himself under the tarp. John capped the jug and dropped it into the sea and got back to studying the strip of water in the boat's shadow. He set up his post at the back of the boat, as far away from JoJo as he could put himself. He had his harpoon ready, but I didn't see any fish except for those small silver ones. They weren't big enough to stab, maybe two inches long. Anyway, all you had to do was think about trying to catch one and they flashed away before your hand hit the water.

"We should have saved a piece of her," John said.

"What are you talking about?"

"Shh. For bait. Just something to keep in mind."

"John? Don't say stuff like that to me, okay?"

"I know it isn't exactly pleasant to think about."

"Gee, really?"

"If it happens, I'm saying. We can't waste anything. If we get enough meat in the water we'll have a good shot at drawing the bigger fish."

"How do you know it won't be you?" I said.

"I don't. And if I'm the first to go, then I want you guys to dig in."

"You're losing it."

"You'd be insane not to, if you could stomach it."

"Now we've gone from bait to food. You could?" I said. "Stomach it?"

"I'd have to."

"You're scaring me, man."

"If that's what it takes to get you to wake up, then a little fear is good."

"I'm awake enough. The panic I felt when the engine conked out—"

"You mean when the supersized zombie over there conked it out," John said.

"Either way, when I looked around and all I saw was black, choppy water? That zing that made me want to puke? That didn't go away, okay? It's become my baseline, and I'm just used to it by now. I'm still plenty scared, so rest easy on that much. I know where we are, what our prospects are."

"I don't think so," John said. "Things are going to have to change if we can't figure out a way to get some food. It could happen before that even, maybe as soon as our water is gone."

"Are you saying you're going to enforce this change, whatever it is you have in mind?"

"I don't have anything in mind. I don't even know what it will look like. I know this, though: I'll have no control over it. None of us will. It'll just happen. And once it starts, there's no going back. No food and the drive to survive can make a person do things he never thought he'd be able to do, especially when he's losing his mind. I'm telling you, Matt, watch your back. Dri's too. As big as he is, I think he might be stronger than he looks."

"And I think you're paranoid."

"Proud to be too."

"We can afford to cut him a little slack here," I said. "The guy just lost the love of his life. He's a wreck. Can you blame him for being a little off?"

"A *little* off? Okay."

"Come on, John. At heart he's a giant teddy bear."

"I don't think you believe that. And if you do, that's the kind of thinking that's going to get you into trouble. I don't know what he is at heart, but it's not a teddy bear. Or if it is, it's one with teeth."

"He cowered just before when you yelled at him about the water."

"We have no choice but to stand up to him out here. You can't show your fear around somebody like that. It triggers something in them. They don't have control over it. They become . . . I don't know. Slaves maybe."

"Slaves to who?"

"Their instinct. Sure, he's cowering—for now. Even he doesn't know he's about to explode. You're not seeing the situation for what it is. You feel sorry for him."

"And that's a problem?"

"When it's messing up your judgment it's a huge problem. Look, we've been here before, and I'm getting tired of it. Why do you always have to put yourself in harm's way? Go wake Dri. It's her time to watch."

"I think you need to take your own advice and get some sleep."

"I'll have to. I just hope you and Dri keep an eye out for me when I do."

And John did sleep, right next to JoJo too, under the tarp. Part of that was the old idea of keeping your friends close and your enemies closer—at least I'm pretty sure that's what John was thinking. Even if he wasn't, he had to hunker under the tarp anyway. The sun was murderous this time of day, four o'clock. Dri had to do her watch duty from the shade of the tent we made from the Windsurfer sail. We'd propped it up on one side with the Windsurfer's fiberglass crossbeam so we had a clear view of the water.

I kept her company and kept watch for her as she tried to rub a twitch out of my shoulder. The dehydration was knotting up the muscles in my back too. Dri dug into my shoulder. It helped, but I didn't want her to burn so many calories on my account. As soon as she stopped the tightness would come back anyway. "Save your energy," I said.

"Doesn't feel good?"

"Awesome. Here, swing around. Your turn."

"No, you can catch me next time," she said. "Bet you're regretting that one now, huh? Giving away those Klondike bars?"

"No. No way."

"Your lips are trembling."

"The rest of me too, I think. It comes in waves. I feel like I'll pass out, and then the feeling passes."

"Me too."

I checked to see if John and JoJo were still asleep. It was so dark under the tarp I couldn't tell. We were far enough toward the back of the boat that John wouldn't have been able to hear me anyway. "It was my fault," I said.

"What was?" Dri said.

"The attack on the car. Mr. Costello. The other night when you tried to make me feel better, when you said I had to understand that we weren't marked, John and I, our dads? We were, and I marked us. It wasn't random at all. I got Mr. Costello killed. Back home he's everywhere, you know? I see him on my way to school, when I turn the corner to catch the train into Manhattan. He's there under the tracks, right where it all went down, lingering in the trestle shadows. He follows me up the steps to the turnstiles. He looks so lost and sad. Like he wants to tell me something, but he can't talk, because his neck is all blown out. His voice is gone."

"And you think you could have stopped the shooting?"

"I could have."

"How?"

"By not starting it. I provoked them, the idiots who were messing with the other team's assistant coach. I practically dared them to fight. I was our catcher. John was pitching. He was our shortstop normally, but both our pitchers were knocked off the mound by then. John was the next best arm. John zips one in. Right when the ump calls 'Strike,' one of the idiots in the bleachers starts howling. His buddies are all coughing, they're laughing so hard. The assistant coach is grabbing at the back of his neck, and he's got clumps of slimy spit between his fingers. I was sick of it. John calls out to me to throw him the ball, but I can't stop staring at the guys who were messing with the assistant coach. The umpire asks me what's up, and I'm just sort of frozen there. John calls me to the mound and I jog out. We come to the conclusion that we need to get rid of these idiots. Now the whole infield's huddling on the mound, and then the outfield jogs in. John and I walk toward the bleachers. We let the idiots know we think it would be a good idea if they left now. I don't have to tell you what they thought of our idea."

"I hate these guys," Dri said. "How can a person find something like that funny? Messing with some poor man who's just trying to take care of his team? If you find that funny, you're not human."

"They're everywhere, though. That's the thing that bums me out the most. I read that one in twenty-five people is a sociopath."

"And this is why you want to run away? You don't think you'll run into people like that in the desert?"

"Less of them."

"Or more. The desert is the perfect hideout."

"Well, these particular psychos, the ones in the bleachers, the last thing they want to do is hide. They want to be seen. They won't leave. They want to be heard. The ringleader calls John and me everything you think he'd call us, and then he tells us to get back out there and play ball, or else. It just burns me, that this guy is going to make all of us stand by while he abuses the assistant coach. Maybe I'm madder because we let it go on so long. That's when the word comes to my lips. I call the ringleader the same thing I'd call myself at this point, a coward.

"Here I'm this fourteen-year-old punk, and this dude's in his thirties, and I'm challenging his manhood. I'm telling him he's afraid to own up to the fact that he's an idiot. If he had the courage to look at himself in the mirror that morning and see himself for the piece of garbage he is, he wouldn't embarrass himself by leaving the house. Well, he's up in my face fast and gives me a double arm shove, and I hit the ground. By now the rest of the team is with us, and there's more shoving, and just when I'm about to get stomped, Mr. Costello gets in there and grabs the ringleader by the ponytail and kicks the back of the guy's knees. Now the ringleader is pinned facedown in the dugout dirt. Mr. Costello *helps* him up. He drags him to the ball-field exit and throws him into the parking lot. As the ringleader and his buddies walk away, I can see him doing it. He's looking back over his shoulder at me and John and most of all Mr. Costello, and he's mumbling to one of his crew. You know the rest."

"John doesn't blame you, does he?"

"No, never."

Dri nodded. "Maybe you're right. I'm not talking about John's dad. You're wrong about that. You were in no way responsible. The only person responsible for the shooting is the shooter. I meant that maybe you were right about John. Maybe he is cool. He went with you to the bleachers to confront the psychopath. He stood by you. He had your back. Matthew, you can blame yourself for one thing only: being awesome. Your dad and Mr. Costello were right to be proud of you. That was beautiful, what you and John did."

"It was reactive," I said. "It wasn't thought out. I gave in to my anger."

"It was good anger. It was justified. You were giving in to your sense of compassion for the man who was being spit on. Somebody had to stand up to those idiots, and you and John did."

Something shrieked. I looked to the sky, but why would an eagle be out here? We turned around and saw John at the mouth of the darker tent, just inside the edge of the shade. He was sitting cross-legged, facing us. He held the sharp end of the harpoon in his lap. He didn't stop looking at us as he filed a notch into the harpoon tip with the side edge of a rusty wrench. Where the chrome plate had chipped away from the wrench the iron was gritty. The fiberglass screeched each time John sawed it. "Can you guys focus on where we are?" John said. "Why do you have to keep dragging it up, Matt? It was three years ago. It has nothing to do with the jam we're in now."

"It has everything to do with now," Dri said. "You two were so brave. You were there for each other."

"Hey," John said to JoJo. "Your phone case. Is it waterproof?"

JoJo didn't seem thrilled with being woken up so suddenly by John's sawing. He mumbled in Portuguese and then said, "My phone case is waterproof, yes, boss. For surfing. Why?"

John nodded to Dri. "Let me see it." She gave him JoJo's phone. The person on watch duty always kept it in case she or he needed to flash the SOS.

John studied the plastic box that covered JoJo's phone. He handed the phone back to Dri. "Can you program the flashlight app to flash once every thirty seconds or so?"

After she did that he looped the phone's safety bracelet around his wrist and lowered the phone into the water.

"What are you doing?" JoJo said. He went right back to scratching himself.

"Fishing," John said. He glared at me over his shoulder. "You think you could stop talking long enough to give me a hand here?

Man the harpoon." We leaned out off the front end of the boat. John lowered his voice. "You feel better now?" He was practically hissing at me. "You got it all off your chest?"

But I hadn't. Not all of it. The phone flash lit up the empty water.

**To:** Lieutenant.Stacy.Quintana@suffolkcountypolice.gov

**From:** Detective.Mark.Kreizler@suffolkcountypolice.gov

**Subject:** DAY 8

**Date:** Wednesday, August 25, 1:45 PM

Both Halloway and Costello were set up with counseling at their middle school after Costello's father was killed. What they said is privileged information, obviously, but the school counselor was able to give me this much: Halloway stopped going after his third session. Costello walked out of the first session, not even five minutes into it, and he never came back.

# 23

*August 26, late morning, the ninth day . . .*

We'd run out of water the day before. The air was cold and damp, but we didn't get any rain. We brushed the dew into the center of the tarp and sail with our hands and ended up with a mouthful each.

JoJo took a picture of himself against the fog. "You said the hunger would go away in a few days, but I'm hungrier than ever," he said.

"John'll catch something today," Dri said. "He will." She tried to stop JoJo from picking at his leg. He batted her hand away. His palm smacked hers so hard he knocked her off balance. That woke him up. He seemed to be as stunned as she was, as we all were.

"Dri, my God, I'm sorry," he said.

Dri played cool, but I saw her pulse in her neck. "It's okay."

"No, seriously, *sinto muito*. I didn't mean it."

"I know you didn't, sweetie pie. Jo, you can't scratch anymore, okay? If you have to, pat it, like Matthew said."

"Of course."

"It'll take the sting out."

"Okay."

"Matthew, maybe you better take another look at it," Dri said.

The wound was beginning to smell. It was moist gray in the middle and red around the edges.

"Matt?" JoJo said. "Is it worse than yesterday?"

"Same."

I'm sure he knew I was lying. All you had to do was take a look at it and you knew there was only one way this thing—a hole in his leg—could go. Deeper. I rebandaged it with the strips of towel I had used on Stef's head. JoJo's blood oozed through what was left of Stef's. He mumbled in Portuguese.

"Matt, Dri, come here," John said. He was at the back of the boat with the binoculars to his eyes. He handed them to Dri. He pointed to where the fog had burned off. "What is that?"

"Where?"

"Way out there. See?"

Dri handed me the binoculars. The water was dark green. Far off was a pale shadow. A pair of gulls circled it.

"Is it?" Dri said.

"Is it what? Please, Matt, let me see," JoJo said. He grabbed the binoculars.

John was leaning over the side of the boat, trying to find the faint wake line. "We're moving away from it." He started the engine. The rumble was louder than I had remembered, the vibrations ringing the boat much more intense. They were wonderful, the sound and feel of a machine after nine days of nothing but wind and wave slaps. And movement. *We* were moving the boat instead of letting it be blown around. The pull of the engine rocked me backward, and I laughed.

"*Terra?*" JoJo said. A tear wiggled through a patch of dried salt on his cheek. "*Terra.*"

Land.

**To:** Lieutenant.Stacy.Quintana@suffolkcountypolice.gov

**From:** Detective.Mark.Kreizler@suffolkcountypolice.gov

**Subject:** REQUEST TO SHIFT SEARCH FOCUS FROM LAND TO SEA, ASAP

**Date:** Thursday, August 26, 11:51 AM

The local police department's call database for August 17 lists an unfounded complaint about a Windsurfer in the vicinity. The complainant's ID was PRIVATE, but I just ran the number. It was Driana.

Here's why I ran the number: Scott Pierce, Gonzaga's neighbor, reported just now that his Windsurfer was stolen, along with his boat. Coast Guard has been notified.

# 25

*Noon . . .*

The land seemed to fade each time we went over a wave. "Is it a mirage?" JoJo said.

"Not if we all saw it," John said.

"John, I'm sliding back into I-really-want-to-like-you-but-can't mode," Dri said. "Can you just be sweet to him? Or how about this: Can you not be nasty?"

The land had vanished, all right, but that was because a wave was blocking our view. Once the wave rolled past the boat, I saw it again. At first I thought it was a few miles away, but it was much closer. The head wind was strong, and the engine groaned as the boat struggled to chop through the waves. We were burning a lot of gas.

The closer we came to the land, the stranger and smaller it looked. It was flat and treeless. When we got even closer I saw it was moving toward us with the waves. They seemed to lift it, a whitish stain in the water. I was pretty sure it was dead seaweed.

It was plastic, a soupy bobbing island of it, bags mostly, soda bottles, laundry detergent containers, all the same bleached gray. I'd read that in the Pacific, patches of this stuff stretch out for hundreds of miles. They're decades old and just beneath the surface. You can't see them from the water. You need satellites to find them. This patch was much smaller, and most of the bottles were intact and floated on the surface. This was a fresh spill. Not fresh enough, though. The ship that dumped the stuff wasn't anywhere in sight. The sun and salt and wind and currents had melded the bags into ropes and clumps. I remembered my textbook for the first responder class. The picture of a body after a head-on car crash. The victim had been ejected from the vehicle, and the intestines hung like streamers from his abdomen.

This was the exact moment JoJo started to turn mean.

He bent over and retched. He didn't have anything in there to throw up. He punched the side of the boat and cursed himself for hurting his hand, and then he punched the fiberglass harder. He glared at John. "We just wasted all that gas. Why are you smiling?"

"We didn't waste it. Look." John pointed to a dead fish caught in the plastic. It was maybe two feet long. I could have been looking at a fresh pizza. I'd been feeling queasy since we left land the week before, but now it was kicking in, that survival instinct John was talking about, the one that could make you do things you didn't think you were capable of, like eating a fish that looked rotten. By the time the carcass hit the floor of the boat a clicking sound had started up in my gut. My own stomach didn't want to be part of me anymore—an alien tired of being locked up in my rib cage. It wanted to crawl up my throat and drop out of my mouth, onto the meat.

My stomach wasn't the only one doing strange things. JoJo's moaned, a ghost from an old movie. He pulled a long scab off his forearm and bled as he watched John size up the fish. "What are you waiting for?" JoJo said.

"It's been dead awhile," John said. "Look at the eyes." They were milky. Scummy threads collected in the gills.

"You're thinking we should throw it back?" I said.

"We're not throwing it back," JoJo said.

"But if we get food poisoning," Dri said.

JoJo cut her off. "Give me the knife."

John eyed JoJo a little too long. He drew the knife he'd made from the Windsurfer's crossbar. He didn't give it to JoJo. He cut into the fish. He worked carefully. We watched him. The skin on John's shoulders had burned, but it was healing now. The blisters had dried and begun to flake away. The patches of new skin were dull reddish brown. His eyes were just as shiny as they always had been, just as black. "I think it might be okay," he said. A half inch in, the meat was pink and then dark red. John trimmed away the rot. The skin and scales were tough, and cutting them away took time.

"This is ridiculous," JoJo said. He elbowed John away from the fish. He grabbed the knife and hacked a chunk out of the fish's belly. He popped it into his mouth and chewed. "It's fine. You've never had sashimi before? Of course you haven't. I forgot whom I was talking to here. Sashimi. Raw fish. You would pay handsomely for this at Kura, if you could afford to go there. Yes, Kura, one of the finest Japanese restaurants in your very own New York City. Never heard of it? Then you will just have to take my word for it." He chopped the fish and pushed pieces at each of us.

"We need to clean away the bad parts," John said. "Only the deep meat is any good. I was going to say I would test it first, until you grabbed yourself a mouthful. I was going to eat a little piece and wait to see if it settled, or if it would make us sick."

"I said it's fine. Eat it." He hacked at the fish and divvied it up. He popped another hunk into his mouth as he worked.

"You need to slow down there, JoJo," John said. "You haven't eaten in more than a week. If you keep gobbling it down like that, it'll come right back up."

JoJo tossed a piece of fish at John. It hit him in the cheek. "Stop talking and start eating your share, before I eat it for you."

"JoJo," Dri said.

"What, Driana? *What?* I'm growing tired of this John here. Why do you always feel you can tell me what to do, John? I mean why do we all listen to you? Why are you in charge? Honestly now, Driana, why have we let him take charge?"

"He knows what he's doing, Jo," Dri said.

"He's a grease monkey. Is that how you say it? Yes, a grease monkey. So if I need my car fixed, I'll summon him. Meanwhile, John, I don't need you to direct me. In fact, let me give you some direction. Back off. Be like your friend here and learn your place."

"So it's like that now," John said.

"It was *always* like that," JoJo said.

"Okay then," John said. "I see."

"No, you don't," JoJo said. "You don't see at all. You *think* you see. Watch yourself, John. You're making me angry."

"Okay," Dri said. "Let's all just take a deep breath."

"No, let's not," JoJo said. "This isn't your meditation yoga class, Driana, with lattes after on the Upper East Side." He nodded to me. "Advise your friend there to leave me alone. You understand me, John?"

"JoJo, please," Dri said. "It's okay. We understand. We do."

"I wasn't *talking* to you, Driana. *Hey,* monkey, I said do you hear me? Then say it."

"I hear you."

"Good. Now keep your mouth shut." He licked the red pulp from his fingers and finished divvying up the fish. He kept a much bigger pile for himself. "I'm twice as big as any of you," he said. "I need more. Here." He tossed the knife near John. "You want it back, right? I'm sure you do." He gathered his meat and slid down the bench, away from us, to the engine, which he used as a table. His skin had become scaly over most of his back and arms. His left shoulder could have been clawed by a bear. His leg was swollen to the point that the skin was about to split along the lines where he'd torn into it, up the length of his shin.

"Should we try it?" Dri said.

We eyed the meat JoJo had left us. John trimmed out the reddest parts. "You know what milk tastes like when it nears the expiration date, just the littlest bit sour?" John said. "If you get a hint of that feeling, make yourself throw up."

We ate. The meat tasted like metal and dirt, but it was fresh enough. I understood why JoJo had wolfed it down. My body wanted the blood in the meat. There was this internal scream happening, a pull in every one of the tens of trillions of cells that had woven together to make me. It was magnetic, my DNA reaching out for the iron in the blood. I forced myself to eat slowly, to chew, to suck out the blood. Pretty soon I wasn't shaking anymore. I'd felt chilled the last few days, no matter how hot it was out there, but now I just felt the heat. My fingers weren't cold anymore. The skin under my fingernails had been pale blue all week. Now it was pink.

A half hour of slow chewing later the meat was gone. John saved the rotten parts and the rest of the carcass and wrapped them in plastic. "Bait," he said. He tucked it into the bottom of one of the cabinets.

"The flies," Dri said.

"No flies out here," John said. "They would have been on the fish already." He lowered his voice. "Or on him." He nodded at JoJo.

"The gulls then," I said. "They'll be dive-bombing us for that stuff."

They hovered high up, directly overhead. John almost smiled at them. "I hope so," he said.

Dri watched the gulls. "Maybe we're near land," she said. "What's their flying range? Anybody know?"

Nobody knew.

JoJo burped. He'd been burping since he started gobbling the fish. He was lying on his back now, under the tarp. He sat up. He leaned over the bow and vomited.

John and I pulled him back in. "Into the boat," I said. "Throw up into the boat."

"Get off me," JoJo said between heaves.

"You're throwing away the meat," John said.

JoJo pounded the bottom of the boat and cursed.

"It's okay, Jo," Dri said.

"Will you stop saying that?" JoJo said.

"I just don't want to see you beat yourself up."

"I'm madder at him than at myself." He nodded John's way. "I'm furious with him for being right. This is insanity. How can it be that I am the first one to fall apart here?" He scratched his shin, and the sore opened up. He screamed but kept digging at the wound. "I'm on fire," he said. "My leg is on fire." Dri reached out to stop him, but I grabbed her arm and eased her away. JoJo slipped into the water and floated on his back. He muttered and cursed and swam off. The wind had pushed the boat away from most of the plastic. A few laundry-soap containers bobbed here and there. I did a double take on a Clorox jug to be sure it wasn't a shark's head.

Dri called to JoJo, but he ignored her. She reached into one of the cabinets for a life vest.

"Wait, I'll go," I said.

"No way," Dri said. "He's not feeling either one of you at the moment."

"Now why would you say that?" John said.

"I know how to calm him down," Dri said. "I know what he needs to hear."

"And what's that?" John said. "That he's not about to turn into a raging psychopath any minute now?"

"That you're not going to hurt him," Dri said. She grabbed another life vest from the cabinet and lowered herself into the water. She swam to him, but not too close. She treaded water. She didn't say anything. He didn't look at her. He stopped cursing and started crying. "I'm staying here," he said.

"I know, sweetie."

"The water feels good."

"I know. But put on the vest, okay?"

"No."

"To save your strength, JoJo. Please."

"*No*, I said."

I knew how he felt. Our skin was burned and raw and the vests chafed. Dri spoke too softly to him for me to hear what she said. He pouted, but he was calming down. He put on the vest and swam away a little farther. Dri followed, and he started talking and crying, and she nodded and stroked his face.

John picked out the bigger chunks of fish from JoJo's vomit. He washed them with seawater and trimmed out the salvageable meat. He watched Dri and JoJo as he worked. "So what do you think about him now?" John said. "It's a one-way trip from here, Matt. He's too far into crazy to make a comeback, and he's becoming our biggest problem."

"When you told me I didn't know when to shut my mouth and when to speak up?" I said. "You were right. Now you need to do the same."

"His wounds are bad. Gangrene. He's dying anyway."

"Not yet, he isn't."

"It can't happen soon enough."

"We better get him out of the water," I said.

"Leave him alone."

"His sores," I said. "All that blood. He'll attract a shark."

"That's what I'm praying for." John studied the notch in his fiberglass harpoon.

# 26

## *DECK LOG, AUGUST 26, 16:21 EST*

**VESSEL:** *USCGC Erica James (WPC 1128), Sentinel-class Fast Response Cutter*

**FROM:** *Navigator, LTJG Nancy Alvarez*

**TO:** *Chief Navigator, Lieutenant David Mercado*

*If their departure point was East Hampton, they were within range of any number of refueling stations. After nine days, they could be in Florida or Nova Scotia. Lieutenant, quick question: where in Hades do you want to start?*

# 27

*Day ten . . .*

JoJo needed a night to cool off before he was able to say he was sorry. Then he needed most of the next day to get himself to mean it. Dri gave him the meat John had salvaged from JoJo's vomit. "He saved it for you, Jo," Dri said.

"Why didn't you eat it yourself?" he said to John.

John looked away. What Dri said wasn't exactly true. Actually, it was exactly a lie. John had been using the meat for bait. He didn't get any takers anyway.

"We need you, Jo," Dri said. "We all have to watch out for each other now. We have to keep our lookout posts too. As many eyes on the sea as possible, right?"

JoJo ate the meat slowly this time. Still, he nearly coughed it up again. His sobbing shook the boat. He pressed in on his eyes with the heels of his hands. "The glare. I feel like someone rubbed broken glass into my eyes. I swear, if I knew it would stop the shimmering, I would blind myself."

"Keep them closed, Jo. Rest. You can take a night watch. You too, Matthew. Your eyes are red. It's my turn to keep lookout."

I settled in near JoJo. I didn't want to, but I was afraid that avoiding him might provoke him. I changed the dressing on his leg. All I could do was scrub out as much pus as I could with the ocean water and use the same filthy strips of towel to cover his wounds. He lifted the dressing and studied his leg.

"Don't," I said.

"I can't anyway," he said. "My fingernails are falling out. What do you think would happen if you made a tourniquet just above the wound, and then John sawed off just below it? I think he would like to do this, no?"

"No, I don't think he'd like that at all, and I know for sure you would end up like Stef."

"Ah, but, Matt, we're all going to end up like Stef. Besides, then we could eat my leg. Only the fresh meat, of course. John will find it. He has shown himself to be quite skillful at trimming away the rot."

"You can't give up, Jo," Dri said.

"But why not?" JoJo said. "Hope is so very draining. It's a bore, actually."

Dri dunked her shirt into the water and wrapped it around JoJo's eyes. She sat by John in the back of the boat and took her turn with the binoculars.

"How you feeling, Jo?" I said.

"Are you serious?" he said.

I tapped his heart. "Here, I mean. What kind of meds were you taking?"

"You're asking me the names of the pills? I can't even remember anymore. One is pink, the other yellow, another light blue."

"You been taking them long?"

"Since I'm fourteen," he said. He laughed quietly. "Yes, finding the right potions, the right doses, took some time. Lots of trial and error. So fun, you know? Not knowing whether the next minute would see me wanting to leap for joy or leap from my balcony. All the while the doctors told me not to lose hope. They said it was the result of a chemical imbalance in my brain. That the way I was feeling wasn't the real me. That I was supposed to feel good—*that* was the natural way of things. But I don't think so, my friend. I think this, here, right now, the way I'm feeling: This is the true me. And I am so very angry. I don't even have the courage to kill myself. Who would build such a world? Tell me. A world where tests like this are commonplace? A monster, no? A sociopath. Who would bring you and Dri together and then crush what might have been? Well, with any luck, you will be allowed to die together. I guess that's something. We must be grateful for minor blessings." He peeked out from under the wrap Dri had put over his eyes. He nibbled at his fingers and sucked at the crusted blood under what was left of his nails. "Good night," he said to me. "Or perhaps it would be better simply to say night." He chuckled and mumbled to himself in Portuguese as he crawled under the tarp.

Dri patted the spot next to her for me to come sit. I joined her and John at the back of the boat. John asked her for the binoculars.

"More plastic?" she said.

"Clouds," he said. But he kept looking at them. "So when were you going to tell me JoJo was on meds, Matt? That he doesn't do so great when he's off them? You too, Dri. You had to be clued in. Didn't it occur to you I might need to know this information?"

"Why?" Dri said. "How's that your business?"

"You're kidding, right?" John glared at her. "I'm sick of all these secrets. Hey, the story Matt told you? Three years ago, the night of the ball game, what happened after? Such a *sad* tale, I know. Poor Matt, poor John especially, right? I want you to know something about Matt, Dri. He flat-out lied to you."

# 28

## *NAVIGATOR'S LOG, AUGUST 27, 12:21 HOURS EST*

*Helicopter searches will stop at sunset, 19:33 hours, per Captain Braswell's orders, after last night's near crash.*

*Tropical storm Carlotta has been upgraded to a Beaufort rating of 10 with sustained winds of 50 knots. NOAA predicts mounting intensity in coming days. It's too early to start using the h-word, but one thing is for sure: This girl is headed our way, folks.*

“It’s time to tell the truth,” John said. He, Dri, and I sat close together in the back of the boat. JoJo was snoring up in the front of the boat, under the heavier tent.

“John, you don’t have to do this,” I said.

“I do.”

“Why? After all these years, we’re going to talk about it now?”

“JoJo was right. One of you could die out here, both of you, all of us. It could happen any minute, the way things are going with big boy over there, with him about to lose what little grip he has on reality. I want to die clean, no lies hanging in the air. I don’t want you thinking of me the way Matt has you thinking of me.”

“What are you talking about?” Dri said. “I’m only thinking good things about you, at least when it comes to that night at the ballpark.”

"Exactly, and that's my point. You're wrong to see me that way."

"You don't think what you did was heroic?" Dri said.

"No, it wasn't. I wasn't. The whole thing was stupid. Look, it didn't happen the way Matt said. What do you call it when you lie not by what you say but by what you don't, by leaving something out of the story, like the most crucial part? My mother used to drag me to church for it and make me confess to the statues."

"A sin of omission," Dri said.

"That's how wrong this feels, letting Matt's version of the story be the one that defines him, me. Sinful. Look, the idiots in the bleachers, the way Matt said they were with Mr. Carlo? That was his name, by the way, the assistant coach. All that stuff was true. The lie starts when Matt told you he ran out to the mound. He did, but I didn't call him out there. That was wishful thinking on Matt's part. He came out on his own. The part about how *we* decided we had to stop the game until the idiots left the ballpark? No. I didn't want to stop the game. I wanted to finish it and get home, before the psychos messing with Mr. Carlo started to get even more psycho and mess with us.

"Matt kept saying that we couldn't leave Mr. Carlo hanging like that. That we had to stick up for him. It was our duty. How could we let this stuff happen right in front of us? How will you sleep tonight? All that garbage. I told him these guys were going to be idiots wherever they were. Us stopping them from spitting on Mr. Carlo wasn't going to stop them from spitting on somebody someplace else. We weren't going to *fix* them or anything, right? I told Matt to get his butt back behind the plate before I kicked it in for him, that the discussion was over.

"Matt grabbed the ball from my mitt and jammed it in his, and now the game was stalled for sure. Yes, Matt marched over to the bleachers and I marched after him. But I followed him to get the ball back and get the game going again, not to have his back. I'm sure it looked like I was right in there with him though. Calling him out to the mound to huddle, like it was my idea in the first place to stand up for Mr. Carlo. Jogging to the bleachers together, standing shoulder to shoulder with my buddy as we faced down the bad guys. Sure, the two heroes. But by the time I was standing there with Matt, he was already mouthing off with the ringleader there. I didn't say a word. Then everything was like he told you—until we stopped at the red light on the way home. Yes, the windows blew in. Yes, they shot my dad. Yes, the nose of the gun came in through the backseat window. But that's where the truth ends."

"John," I said, but he cut me off.

"Shut up, man. Ever wonder why Matt was shot in the back, Dri? He covered me. The shooter was aiming at me, and Matt put himself between us. He took my bullet. You wondered how I survived the car crash that came after that without a scratch, right? All those tools flying around? It wasn't any miracle. It's because I wasn't in the car. I kicked the door open and ran. I left my father and my best pal bleeding in my dad's crummy old secondhand van, and I took off as fast as I could. And you know what? I was right to run. What else could I do? They had guns, I had nothing. I was right about Mr. Carlo too. It was none of our business. He was going to get picked on wherever he went. How is that my fault? I liked him a ton, and I admired him, but it wasn't my job or *duty* or whatever to get myself killed for him."

"Why are you doing this?" I said to John. "Why do you have to make yourself out to be the bad guy?"

"I'm not saying I was the bad guy," John said. "I tried to stop you from getting yourself into a mess. If that makes me bad or a coward, I don't care. The label means nothing to me. I was right to do what I did that night, to try to hold you back, to save myself when I got the chance, and I would do it again, just the same way. My eyes are shot. I need to sleep. Wake me when it gets dark. I'll probably wake up anyway." He gave me the binoculars and lay on his back under Dri's tent, the one we made of the sailcloth.

Dri's eyes looked less green and more violet, reflecting the change in the water's color. The clouds were coming. She pointed to the darker tent.

JoJo was awake. He was sitting up at the edge of the tarp, looking at himself in his phone screen. He chuckled and stuck out his tongue. Pale brown gunk coated it. A crack was beginning to form down the middle. He took a selfie with his tongue out. *Click*. "I don't know why we have sound effects on our phones," he said.

"There's no real clicking here. Why do we need the lie? Right, John?" He checked the picture and nodded. "We should get it over with. We should die with what little dignity we have left. We should kill ourselves."

Dri took the phone from him and put it into the cabinet.

# 30

*Afternoon, day eleven . . .*

The sky was more clouds than blue, and JoJo's calf was red. It was hot to the touch and swollen. The skin was beginning to rip outward from the wound in a starburst pattern not too different from the one on my shoulder, except that his was shiny with pus. Looking at it made me wince, but JoJo was done being embarrassed by it. He called it *my friend here.* As in, "My friend here would like a sip of seawater. Won't you fetch me some, Matt?"

That was all I could do, drizzle seawater over it, knowing this was doing nothing except cooling it temporarily. I double bagged the filthy dressings. I was going to throw them overboard to get rid of the stink.

"Wait," John said. He threw the rotten fish carcass in with the rags and poked the bag full of small slits. He tied off the bag and hung it so it trailed us just below the water's surface.

"We could use a hook right about now," I said. "Can't you cut one out of the fiberglass from the Windsurfer mast?"

"It's too brittle. It'll crack. The best I can do is a notch. That'll be enough to keep the point in there. All we have to do is draw big boy near enough where we can spear him." He filed the tip of the harpoon he'd made from the Windsurfer mast with the rusty wrench.

"I'm thinking of what your mom told us that time we went camping," I said, "when we tried to help that bear cub after that moron's Winnebago ran over its paw. 'Be careful about what you chase. You just might catch it.' "

"The time *you* tried to help it," John said. "I said let it be. I'm not afraid of dying, Matt. I'm afraid of not doing everything I can to stay alive. We need two lookouts now, round the clock. One watches for fish, another for ships, while the third rests."

I didn't bring up the fact that there were four of us. JoJo hadn't pulled a watch in two days. He'd gone quiet, but not in any way that gave me the feeling he was less likely to explode. He seemed to be plotting something. He muttered in Portuguese.

"What was that, sweetie?" Dri said.

JoJo shrugged. "Nothing." His eyes ticked to John and then back to his wound. His smile was creepy and sad at the same time, the kind you see on somebody who has nothing to lose.

John lifted the bait bag out of the water and put a few more slits into it. I smelled it in the wind, the iron in the blood.

"Where is a shark when you need one, eh?" JoJo said. "Now *he* would do it. *He* would be a good friend and chop off my leg for me."

Dri stopped telling him to stop talking that way.

Dri and I always tried to be touching somehow, shoulder to shoulder, knee against knee, hand in hand. She drew soft circles into my palm with her fingertips. This wasn't an attempt at romance. It was deeper than that. Her touch was the only thing that seemed real out there. The rest of it was a bizarre slow-motion thrill, which didn't make it any less painful or confusing. I couldn't have imagined that I, a kid whose closest contact with boating was the Staten Island Ferry when I visited my aunt once a year, would end up lost at sea. Now I was beginning to wonder if I could go back to the land with these eleven days adrift in my memory. The two worlds seemed too separate to bring one back into the other without some kind of trouble following, except I was beginning to think I wasn't going to have to worry about that now.

The ships that had come close enough to us were too fast to chase. The ones that came at night, when they were lit up and easier to see, were out of our gas-supply range. We had maybe five minutes of drive time left in the tank. That would move us three miles or so—less if we were driving against wind and waves. The freighters didn't see us or must have thought we were fine. We had no way to advertise we were in trouble, no radio to call the Coast Guard, no flares. Our SOS flashes were lost either in the sun or moon glint apparently. Nobody had any idea where we were. How could they? Even if they figured out we'd borrowed the boat by now, why would we have stayed on the water?

Then again, how could we not be on the water? If we'd come back on land we would have gone home. Why would five kids who didn't know one another simultaneously decide to run away for a week and a half, without leaving a single word with loved ones? The only logical conclusion was that we'd gotten into trouble and drowned.

Would we? Was that how it would end? Would we capsize in a storm? Drowning would have been preferable to dying of thirst. What would *that* look like? How would it feel? Would it be so painful that there would be a need for mercy killing? Would the dried-out dying beg for death? And what about the last survivor? Who would put him out of his misery, or her? No, it would be John, I was sure, as sure as I was that I wouldn't be able to watch Dri die. I'd want to go first—but after JoJo. I couldn't leave her with him, or what was left of him. Watching him sleep under the tarp, I had a good picture of how he would die. Acute systemic infection, the same thing that had killed Stef probably. That was if John didn't get to him first.

John slept in Dri's tent or pretended to sleep. His eyes were closed but he'd stopped sleeping in his vampire pose, with his hands folded over his chest. Now they were at his hips, where he kept his homemade knife.

Dri was on the lookout for ships, nodding off. She'd barely said a word after John gave her the true story about Woodhull Road. I let her sleep. She wasn't missing anything anyway. The horizon and water leading out to it were empty. I was supposed to be on the lookout for fish. I was nodding off myself when I heard a splash on the side of the boat. At first I thought it was a wave that had slapped the fiberglass, but the sound had a squeaky click in it.

It was much smaller than the one that flipped Stef's Windsurfer. Maybe it weighed fifty pounds. This one looked like the kind I'd seen in movies, pale gray. It didn't have any interest in the bait. It swam alongside the boat, touching it side to side. I shook Dri's shoulder. "A dolphin," I whispered.

Dri leaned out over the bow with me to watch it. "She's a porpoise. See how her nose is rounded?"

"She looks sick," I said. The porpoise kept sinking and then flicking her tail to come back flank to flank with the boat.

"She's a baby," Dri said. "She lost her mom, I bet. Porpoises get caught in fishing nets all the time. They don't like to travel alone."

The harpoon sank into her just behind her head. The porpoise thrashed and swam away with the harpoon stuck in her. She swam out the short length of the rope John had tied to the boat's railing. The rope jerked tight and bent the railing, and we lost our footing.

The boat rocked low into a wave and took in water. At first I thought JoJo was crying, but he was laughing.

John yanked on the line and pulled the porpoise close enough to where I could help him drag her into the boat. She flopped and bucked and the harpoon swung wildly. John and I tackled her.

"How could you do that?" Dri said.

"How could you not?" John said. "What's wrong with you two, sitting there, watching the thing? I thought you were going to pet it. Wake up. Give me the hammer. Come on, so I can put it out of its misery."

Dri pulled the hammer from the bench cabinet. John swung down on the porpoise's skull, but it was thrashing so much he only got in a glancing shot.

The porpoise kicked up with its tail. John swung down again, and this time he connected. I heard a popping sound, and then another one when John swung the hammer into the porpoise's temple. The porpoise writhed and bucked and flopped right out of the boat. It dove and stretched the line. The boat rocked down again, and we took on more water. John pulled out the slipknot to release the line, and the boat rocked back up. The rope ran out and whipped into the water and then we lost sight of it.

"Bail," John said. "Bail and get the paddles."

We bailed, the three of us. John and I scooped with the tarp and Dri used the milk crate setup.

“And you thought you were going to catch a shark?” JoJo said. “Yes, Dri, you were right. John certainly knows what he is doing after all.”

I spotted the harpoon a few hundreds yards away. It poked up straight from the water and then went under and poked up again a few yards farther off, and then it sank fast. We paddled after it, but we never saw it again.

“No dignity,” JoJo said. His laughter faded. “I am telling you, the only thing to do now is take that little knife John has there and . . .” He drew his index finger across his neck. He picked up the hammer and measured its weight. Dri took it out of his hand and he started laughing again, so hard he cried.

# 31

## *NAVIGATOR'S LOG, AUGUST 29, 10:59 HOURS EST*

*Last night we made contact with two crews who said they might have seen the kids. Further investigation proved these sightings were of the same vessel, but it was a fishing boat. Folks are beginning to wonder just how much longer Uncle Sam is going to foot the bill for this misadventure.*

# 32

*Day twelve . . .*

John lifted the bait bag from the water. The meat hadn't been touched. JoJo watched. "At what point does it enter your mind that catching anything with that isn't a remote possibility?"

John dropped the bag into the water and got back to his lookout. The heel of his hand rested on his knife.

"We're in empty waters, *John*. Dead water." JoJo slipped into the water and floated on his back.

"JoJo, wear a vest," Dri said.

He ignored her and floated off.

"That harpoon would have worked if he'd helped and not just sat there," John said. "The porpoise. All Lurch had to do was fall on the thing. Look, he said he wants to die, right? And he keeps saying it. We need to be proactive here. When you know it's coming, why wait to get hit?"

"I don't think I want to know what that means," I said.

"You already know what it means, Matt. Like you haven't thought about it too? Give me a break. You want to wait for him to flip out with the hammer? You might as well hand it to him. It's going to happen sooner or later."

"Jo can't hear you, but I can," Dri said.

"I want you to hear me," John said. "The three of us. We have to be together on this."

"His wounds will kill him first," I said.

"Then if he's dead anyway, why not put him out of his misery? Dri, Matt's in if you are."

"I didn't say that," I said.

"But it's true," John said. "I can tell by looking at you. You know I'm right."

"No, I don't. I have mixed feelings."

"Pick one," John said. "One way or the other. Just make a decision."

"He's not himself," Dri said. "I know him, and this isn't JoJo."

"Well, whoever he is, he's about to go psycho on us. We have one option here, and the longer we wait to exercise it, the more we put ourselves at risk."

"Do you really want it that bad, John?" Dri said.

"Want what? I have nothing against him."

"You do, but I'm not talking about that. I mean do you really want to be the last one left? To die alone?"

"We wouldn't be out here if it wasn't for you. The three of you. For all your money, you're idiots. I'm trying to make the best of a rotten situation."

"The best?" Dri said. "Are you for real? How do you want to do it, John? No, seriously, I want to know. Are you going to choke him? Cut him?"

"One shot to the head with the hammer. That's all it'll take."

"Right, because that worked so well with the porpoise," Dri said.

"It was squirming around. I couldn't get in a solid shot. He'll be sleeping. We do it then, nice and quiet. He won't suffer."

" 'We,' huh? No." Dri wiped away her tears. "I'm not crying for Jo. I'm crying for you. You have no faith, John."

"Faith in *what*?"

"*Any*thing. You tried to keep Matt from standing up for Mr. Carlo."

"That's right. You bet I did. And what's that got to do with this anyway?"

"You want to kill Jo?" she said. "Then do it, but don't be a sneak about it. Tell him you're going to do it. Tell him to his face."

"You really are losing it, Dri," John said. "Maybe that's how it plays out in one of those fairy-tale philosophy books you read in prep school, some fantasy of morality, but we're a long way from there."

"I know where I am," she said. "I know exactly. And I'm not so lost that I don't know *what* I am too."

"And what's that?"

"Still human."

In all our time on the water, that was as close as John came to full-out laughter. "Human, huh? Human means something else to me."

"I know what it means to you," she said.

"You're not human," John said. "You have enough money that you don't have to be human. You can pretend to be while you let the rest of us do the dirty work. You're a spoiled little brat, and you're way out of your element."

"And you're a coward."

"Okay, I'm a coward then, fine." He tightened the rag on the handle of his fiberglass knife to give it a better grip.

"Could you actually do it, John?" Dri said. "Could you muster the guts to kill him? I don't think so. I mean, I know you're more than willing to sit back when somebody else does it, to run when the shots are fired, but could you swing that hammer yourself? We're not talking about some defenseless baby porpoise here. We're talking about a real live human being. Could you look him in the eye and then take him out?"

"Dri, look *me* in the eye," John said. "Yes. Yes, I could, and I will, if it comes to that. I don't want to, but if I have to, it's a done deal, no problem whatsoever for me." He went back to his fishing.

"This is a mistake, not coming together on this. We should have done it yesterday. Every minute we let him be this way, we're giving him permission to kill us."

"What exactly is he doing that tells you he's about to go on a murder spree?" Dri said.

"Aside from taking more than his share of the meat and saying that if we had any dignity we'd slit our throats? He isn't doing anything at all, and that's the even bigger problem. We're all smacking ourselves to stay awake and keep a lookout for a ship, and he laughs at us. We collect the dew off the tarp in the mornings, and he drinks it. We distill and he waits to be served."

"He can't do anything anyway with his leg the way it is," Dri said.

"He can't keep *watch*? Where's the heavy lifting in that? He's deadweight, and he's going to take us down with him. He's used to having all the power, and the only power he has now is to let us live or die."

"I could see him killing himself," I said, "and I wouldn't blame him for it. But why would he take us down with him?"

"Why did those dudes shoot into my father's van? He's built that way. At heart, that's who he *is*. Sure, he's everybody's pal when things are easy, but turn up the heat a little, and now you're seeing the real JoJo."

"Even if you were right—and you're not—he couldn't hurt us if he wanted to," Dri said. "He couldn't hurt himself at this point."

"He came on here weighing close to three hundred pounds, I'd say. Maybe he's down to two seventy, and the thirty pounds he burned were water and fat. We're *all* weaker than we were twelve days ago. It takes just one last explosion, and there's nothing we can do to stop him. The fiberglass creaked when he punched it. I thought he was going to put a hole in the boat."

"You don't know him," Dri said.

"Neither do you. You know a medicated version of him who's got you fooled—who had himself fooled until now. I'm telling you, he's going to pop."

"So what are you going to do at this point, John?" Dri said. "Is this one of those 'If you ain't with me, you're against me,' things? You gonna take us out too?"

"No, I'm just going to keep trying to catch you some dinner, princess. And I'll keep watching your back too, if only for Matt." He hit me with those black eyes. "I'm not asking you to side with me over her here. I'm asking you to stand tall for yourself and wake up before it's too late."

"If we do this, we'll never be able to get rid of it," Dri said. "I'm saying if somehow we're rescued, we're still damned."

"Now you're scared of going to hell? News flash: You're floating in it. You're starting to worry me more than JoJo is right about now, bringing God into this. Just look at us. You think anybody's watching what we're doing?"

"I'm scared of what I become if I murder somebody," she said.

"It's self-defense."

"It's murder," Dri said. "You're not touching him, John. I'll kill you first."

JoJo screamed. At first I thought he'd overheard us, but he was twenty yards out and upwind of us. He was swimming for the boat. I'd never seen him move so fast. He stopped swimming to kick at something in the water. The water angled up and then dropped with a wave, and I saw it.

Its tail wasn't flipping up and down the way the dolphin's had, or even the baby porpoise's. It was switching side to side.

# 33

**To:** Lieutenant.Stacy.Quintana@suffolkcountypolice.gov

---

**From:** Detective.Mark.Kreizler@suffolkcountypolice.gov

---

**Subject:** DNA SAMPLE CAME BACK ON BODY PART FOUND BY TRAWLER

---

**Date:** Sunday, August 29, 7:29 PM

---

It was Estefania Gonzaga. Permission to transfer case status from Missing Persons to Homicide?

# 34

*Hazy sunset, day twelve . . .*

The shark didn't seem to be in attack mode. It circled JoJo slowly. It was longer than the dolphin that flipped Stef's Windsurfer, maybe by two or three feet, but it wasn't as thick. It probably weighed as much as the dolphin. Still, I couldn't stop myself from remembering just how much damage the dolphin caused without using a single tooth. JoJo screamed and cursed as the shark's circles tightened.

We paddled the boat toward JoJo almost as fast as he swam toward us. The shark moved lazily until JoJo kicked its flank. Its body snapped into a C, almost like it was about to bite its own tail. Then it went under. The fin came up and moved fast, first away from JoJo and then right back at him.

I swung out a paddle to JoJo. Dri wrapped her arms around my waist to anchor me. JoJo grabbed the paddle. Just like in the movies, the shark went for the leg first, the bloodiest candy. Its mouth opened and then the hammer struck the top of its head.

John swung down a second time, but the shark was gone. We helped JoJo into the boat. He was so freaked out he pulled me into the water as he tried to pull himself out of it. I don't think I was in the water for more than a couple of seconds. John and Dri yelled for me to grab their hands, but I didn't need any help. I pulled up on the bow of the boat and flung myself into it, no problem. My guts burned from the adrenaline surge. I would have wet myself if I had any water in my bladder. The rush of energy buzzed through me and settled in the roots of my teeth. My molars felt like they were going to crack. I tasted metal.

"It's okay," Dri said. "We're all okay."

JoJo yelled at her in Portuguese. I got that he was telling her to stop saying that. That we definitely were not anywhere in the vicinity of okay. He grabbed her shoulders and shook her. His fingertips were deep into the skin on her arms. She groaned and tried to peel away his hands. She scratched at a sore on his shoulder. He screamed and flung her off. Her head smacked the bench cabinet. Blood drops hit the water on the boat deck and spread out like exploding red stars. JoJo stepped toward Dri.

It had all happened so quickly, or too quickly for me to realize I had to stop it, but now the fear that had come from being in the water a few feet away from a shark was being replaced by the fear that JoJo was so out of his mind that he was going to kill Dri. I pushed between them and drove the heels of my hands into JoJo's chest. A shockwave lit up my left arm from my wrist into my elbow, like I'd punched concrete. JoJo came back at me with a fist to my shoulder. The force of the punch tumbled into my spine, my legs. That one shot took me off my feet. I hit the floor of the boat hard enough to see stars, except they looked more like bits of electric static. The sky was a grainy video, fuzzy streaks of clouds against a speckled, hyper-blue background. John put himself between JoJo and us, hammer raised.

Dri begged, "Please, stop." I don't know whether she was talking to John or JoJo or both, but neither seemed to hear her.

JoJo wasn't focused on us anymore. He was looking out into the water. He pointed out the shark and hyperventilated. The shark circled the boat slowly. It was well beyond arm's reach, too far away to get hit with a hammer, but close enough that I saw notches in its fin.

I had rolled over onto my hands and knees to watch the shark. The adrenaline was washing out of me, and I was so dizzy I started to fall when I tried to stand. The best I could do was sit, my back against the side of the bench seat cabinet. I wanted to throw up, but of course my stomach was empty. Dri was checking out my scalp. Her fingers combed through my hair. She was freaked. "You whacked your head really hard," she said.

"You too," I said. Her hand was bloody.

"No," she said. "I cut my finger when I grabbed the edge of the bench to break my fall." The bench seats that battened the cabinets were plastic and chipped. She showed me the wound. It wasn't bad, a nick in her fingertip.

"You hit your head too though," I said. "I heard a *bock*."

"So did I," John said.

"No," Dri said. "My head hit the seat cushion. The sound was from when my hand smacked the bench to break my fall. The cover popped back up a little." She looked toward JoJo. "He's totally insane," she whispered to me or maybe to herself, I don't know, but John heard her. "He's *been* totally insane," he said.

JoJo was pale and sweaty. He shivered and chattered to himself and pulled his hair as his eyes tracked the shark.

"You still believe in God, Dri?" John said. "Because that right there was the answer to our prayers."

Dri ignored John. "Jo?"

"Why'd you pull him out?" John was talking to me now. He was right up in my face, so JoJo wouldn't hear. Not that JoJo would have been able to hear anything but his own moaning. It was so loud the boat vibrated with it, an ugly hum in the fiberglass.

"JoJo?" Dri said.

"Two birds, one stone, Matt. He dies and we wouldn't have blood on our hands. *Idiot*." John eyed the shark. "We're stuck with that thing now, you know? It's ours. Yes, we have a nasty hammer, but no way it's just going to swim away from a boat full of meat."

"You should be happy," Dri said. "All you've been doing the past week is trying to draw one to the boat."

“That was when I had a harpoon,” John said. He dropped the hammer and went to the bow and pulled the bait bag out of the water.

“Hey,” I said to John. “Why’d you hammer it?”

“What?”

“You’re yelling at me for pulling JoJo out of the water, but you’re the one who saved him. Why?”

“Because . . . I don’t know.” John tore the bait bag from the towline and threw it as far away from the boat as he could.

“Matthew, let me see your eyes.” Dri put her thumb tips to my eyelids and lifted them and leaned close to look into my pupils.

“I’m okay,” I said.

“I don’t think so,” John said. “None of us are.” He nodded JoJo’s way.

JoJo had curled up into a ball. He put his fists to his mouth and screamed.

# 35

*Three hours until daylight, day thirteen . . .*

Light rain woke me—more like nudged me out of my daze. I didn't dare sleep now.

Dri and I helped John funnel the rainwater off the tarp into the gas jug. The rain didn't wake JoJo. He was balled up on the floor by the engine, where he had conked out.

We'd grabbed a bunch of laundry detergent bottles from the garbage spill, but we didn't need them. We collected half a jug before the rain stopped. Still, it was enough to fill our shrunken stomachs. We took turns drinking and keeping an eye on JoJo.

After he'd calmed down, he cried for what seemed an hour. He'd genuinely seemed not to remember shoving Dri or punching me. "*I* did that?" he'd said when Dri told him what happened. After that he crawled to the back of the boat and collapsed. We hadn't heard from him since, except for his snoring, which must have been painful for him. It sounded like when boiling water rattles the pot cover.

Dri peeked into the jug. Maybe a third of what we'd collected was left. She looked to where JoJo was sleeping.

"Don't," John said. "Please don't."

"If he wakes up and finds out we have water and didn't offer him any . . . I don't know."

"That's why we should drink it all right now," John said.

"That sound," she said. "His throat must be so dry it's cracking."

"Leave him alone, I'm telling you," John said.

She ignored him and brought the jug to JoJo. I went with her. I was ready to knock JoJo into the water if he so much as gave her a dirty look, and I wasn't going to pull him back into the boat this time. I couldn't see the shark with daylight still a few hours away, but I felt it there, gliding along just on the other side of the fiberglass, this starving presence.

We had a hard time waking JoJo up, but when he came to, he drained the jug, of course. He muttered thanks but sarcastically, as if he resented our help. Then he mumbled to himself as he went to work picking at his skin. He started in on a boil on his shoulder. His fingernails were gone, so he rubbed his shoulder against the side of the boat. He grunted as he scraped. "Matt, get the light?" he said. "I want to see."

I was about to tell him he really didn't want to see, that none of us did. I was afraid he'd flip out when he saw what I was pretty sure was going to be a rotting hole in his shoulder. I couldn't risk making him mad, though, so I got the phone out of the cabinet and shined the light on his shoulder.

I was wrong. The wound wasn't rotting. It was a fresh two-inch pit. I winced at the sight of the raw skin hanging from his shoulder. He twisted his neck to see what he had done to himself. He kicked down on the fiberglass with his heels. The boat vibrated.

I heard a splash off the left side of the boat, and then another on the right. I shined the light into the water. There were two sharks now.

JoJo went back to picking at his skin. Dri didn't tell him to stop. He eyed John and growled and laughed quietly to himself.

John didn't flinch. He didn't provoke either. He looked away and put the binoculars to his eyes and scanned the horizon for lights, or pretended to.

"Look up," JoJo said. He was talking to me. "Look."

The sky was clearing strangely. The edge of a high-pressure band pushed the clouds away in a perfectly straight line. JoJo pointed to the stars. "The Hercules Cluster," he said. "See?"

I didn't see it, but I said, "Sure, right there. Cool."

"He was a Roman invention, stolen from the Greeks and cleaned up, made more Hollywood, if you will. The original Greek version of the myth was much grimier, and so much closer to my heart. They called him Heracles. He is my kinsman. You have no idea what I am talking about, do you?"

He didn't either, I thought, but he had enough mental power left to give me one last lesson in tragedy. "Heracles was made to wear a poison robe that ate away his flesh," he said. "To end his suffering he begged to be thrown into the fire, but no one would do it. They were cowards. All of them."

Dri tried to hold his hand, but he nudged it away, and then I nudged her away from him.

One by one they fell asleep—first JoJo, then John, then Dri. That was always the order when I was on watch. Dri couldn't sleep until she was sure John wasn't going to attack JoJo, and John couldn't sleep until he was sure JoJo wasn't going to attack him. Dri slept with the hammer.

I saw a freighter's lights on the horizon. I didn't bother to wake anyone. Why get their hopes up? Still, I reached into the cabinet for JoJo's phone and flashed the ship. The light was weak, and the ship was far away. Ten minutes later the boat dropped back under the horizon, and the sky clouded over fast.

The waves were beginning to get bigger. They rocked me into a daze. My head weighed a hundred pounds. It dropped, and I slapped myself awake. I had another half hour before my watch was over. Dri was due to take the next shift, but I wished it were John's turn. I half hoped John would kill JoJo while Dri and I were asleep. I wondered—if Dri stood up to John, would he take her out too? He knew he would have to kill me first. Would he? Could he kill me after what we went through together that night on Woodhull Road? The times after that, when my family had his back?

I was nodding off when Dri relieved me. She was groggy. I wanted to stay with her to help keep her awake. She insisted she was okay, that as bad as she looked, I looked worse and needed to get some sleep. I did, too. I was shivering. The air was coldest at this hour, a couple of hours before dawn.

I settled in under the tarp we'd restrung at the front of the boat. John snored quietly. My shivering exhausted me, and I fell asleep fast. I don't know how long I was out when I felt the boat rock and then I heard a splash. I was groggy. I needed a few seconds to remember where I was and to realize that John wasn't under the tarp anymore. Then I heard Dri scream.

# 36

*August 30*

*Dear Senator Rice,*

*I understand that with the discovery of my niece Estefania Gonzaga's partial remains, the Coast Guard is considering calling off the search for the remaining young people lost at sea the night of August 17. I implore you to ask Admiral Sutterjee to reconsider this decision. I will do everything I can to finance a continued search.*

*Please, Mark. I beg you, ask the admiral to give the kids one last shot.*

*Sincerely,*
*Rafael Gonzaga*

# 37

*Dawn . . .*

JoJo was gone. Dri and John scanned the water. "What happened?" John said.

"You didn't see?" Dri said.

"You were on watch," John said.

Dri cursed herself. "I nodded off," she said. "How could I do that? How could I desert him like that? He needed to be looked after."

"The splash that woke me up," John said. "I think it came from the left."

Sure enough, JoJo rose to the surface not far from where John pointed. He groaned.

There were four sharks after all. JoJo was jerked down, but he didn't go all the way under. Blood spread out from him. He looked confused. He stared at John as a shark bit his shoulder and shook him to tear away the skin. He didn't have time to scream before another shark clamped its mouth over his head. Tail fins whipped the water into pink froth. I think the sharks started to attack one another too. I had to sit. My legs went weak and I plunked down on the bench seat. Dri sat next to me and dry heaved. John stood tall and kept looking into the water. He nodded for a while. Then he looked at Dri and me and nodded some more.

Maybe a few minutes passed before Dri's stomach settled and I noticed a light was strobing weakly in the morning glare. JoJo's phone was on the floor of the boat, in the corner. It blipped S-O-S.

"Happy now?" Dri said.

"Sure, Dri," John said. "I'm having the time of my life."

Half an hour later we three were lying back against the boat walls. We needed that much time to paddle and drift away from the blood trail, to realize that for the first time in several days we could breathe a little more freely. The sense of relief was as huge as the sense of sadness I felt about the way JoJo died. I knew him for two intense weeks, long enough to know John was wrong about him. The JoJo of the last few days wasn't the real João Martins. The JoJo I'd remember was that nice guy I met on the beach. The one who wanted to take us surfing.

The morning air felt more like the afternoon, when it was so hot you didn't want to move. I was burning up. I didn't see any sharks, but they couldn't be too far away with all that blood around. I checked the sea on all sides before I dared reach down to scoop a little water onto my face. The clouds were black and moved fast, but where the sun broke in, the rays wriggled through my skull.

I couldn't stop thinking about the look on JoJo's face right before the sharks attacked. He was smiling, and he was looking at John.

Dri leaned into me and flashed through the pictures on JoJo's phone. They started with the party at Dri's. Stef stuck her tongue out at the lens. Then there was John, checking out Mr. Gonzaga's new Porsche. There was one of Dri and me, holding hands by the pool.

"Save the battery," John said. "Turn it off." I did and stowed the phone in the cabinet under the bench seat. The waves were getting bigger, and JoJo's phone was our last chance at getting out an SOS flash. John's battery had died the day before. I looked around the boat for loose items that needed to be secured. I put the distiller in there, the peanut can, the empty water jugs. I forced myself to pretend I wasn't scared when I asked, "Where's the hammer?"

Dri pointed to where she slept, but it wasn't there.

"I have it," John said. He pulled it from his sleeping spot under the tarp. "What do you need it for?"

"I don't," I said.

"Quit looking at me that way, Matt. Until he did us the favor of killing himself, I wasn't taking any chances."

"I bet you weren't," I said.

"Here, you know what?" He tossed the hammer into the ocean.

"What'd you do that for?" Dri said.

"In case we turn on each other. Isn't that what you guys are afraid of? That I might hit you while you're sleeping?"

"Actually, John, no," Dri said. "Not until you mentioned it."

John pulled out three life vests and started to tie them down to the railings. He left them open in the front so we could buckle ourselves into them.

"What are you doing?" Dri said.

"They're seat belts," John said.

"Okay, and we need them because?"

"So we don't get thrown from the boat. Look." He pointed toward the horizon, except there wasn't a horizon anymore. The water and sky were the same color, almost black, and all I could think about was JoJo, how lucky he was to miss what was coming.

# 38

*Late afternoon, day thirteen . . .*

The waves didn't break, and the clouds didn't either. The sun wasn't supposed to set for another hour, but night came early that day. Overhead was a dark purple skin with gray veins. It slid over the sky with a definite edge, God's eyelid closing. It stretched out to the horizon in every direction.

We'd strapped ourselves in at the back of the boat, John on one side, Dri and me on the other. John actually slept. He hadn't in days, I think, afraid JoJo would wring his neck the minute he nodded off. It was so ridiculous I actually laughed. Here he was snoring away in a modified vampire pose—how a vampire would sleep sitting up—and we were about to get hit with a storm strong enough to sink the boat, it looked like. Dri laughed with me. Then in the space of a breath Dri's laughing stopped, and she looked so sad. Her hair beads had chipped and faded from blue to white. Her eyes were dark, picking up the purple in the sky. "You think he did it," she said. "You think John killed JoJo." The way she said it, she definitely wasn't asking.

John's head swung loosely with the waves. For a second I thought he was dead, until I saw his chest rise and fall.

"You don't?" I said.

"No way. It was suicide. John wouldn't have the courage."

"He would," I said. "He does. You don't know him. You don't know what he's capable of. He's the most fearless guy I know."

"You can't be serious. He runs from every fight, and he admits to it. He's *proud* of it."

"Not the hardest fight," I said. "The most important one. He's been pretty much supporting his mom since he was fourteen. After Mr. Costello was killed, she drank to the point she couldn't work. He goes with her to her rehab counselor. He makes *sure* she goes."

"Matt, do you hear yourself?" she said. It was the first time she hadn't called me Matthew. "Why didn't you tell me this stuff before?"

"He'd be mad if he knew I told you."

"Why?"

"He doesn't want people knowing he's a good guy."

"That makes no sense."

"He doesn't want to ask anybody for anything, you know? Even if it's just to feel good about him. John can tough out anything, and he'd kill somebody to keep himself going, to keep his mom going."

"This is awful. The two of you. I don't know what to do here. Please, you have to believe me. JoJo killed JoJo. He'd been battling depression for a long time. John is . . ."

"What?"

"He's your brother."

"That's right, and I know him better than anybody. Brothers or not, if he thought I was a danger to him, he'd kill me too."

"How do I get you not to think this way?" She kissed my eyes and then my lips. Her skin was sticky. Her lips were salty and chapped. We kissed and kissed, and all the while John Costello's head swung loose, like the life had gone out of it, rocking back and forth with the waves that were starting to throw the boat.

# 39

## ***NAVIGATOR'S LOG, AUGUST 31, 05:51 HOURS EST***

*Ladies and gentlemen, prepare to meet Carlotta. At present, her waves are topping forty feet.*

# 40

*Sunless sunrise, day fourteen . . .*

The waves beat us up all night, but the rain didn't come until morning. It came warm and smoky at first, and then it turned cold and fell harder and didn't let up. We popped out of our life-vest seat belts to catch the rainwater with the tarp. Even the storm waves and the threat of being thrown overboard couldn't scare off our thirst. We didn't need more than a few minutes to fill the jugs. We strapped back into our seat-belt vests and passed the jug around. I drank too fast; we all did. I felt weak and loose in my limbs, but Dri's head was bobbing and then swinging as lifelessly as John's had the night before.

"How does she pass out from drinking water?" John said.

"Too much water. I should have stopped her. Hyponatremia, it's called. They told us about it in that first responder class. It's what happens to distance swimmers and marathoners after they finish and they're dehydrated, and then they guzzle water. It dilutes the salt in their blood and knocks everything out of whack."

"How do we fix it?"

"We don't, unless you happen to have a quart of Gatorade on you. Her blood will balance out on its own, I think. How soon, though, I don't know."

"Not soon enough. Hang tight to her. Matt, brace her."

A wave two stories high rolled up on us and ripped the boat into its crest, and then the sea dropped. My stomach lifted and I was dizzy as we coasted down the back of the wave.

"You have to brace her better," John said. "Her head's whipping all over the place. She'll break her neck."

I held her close to keep her head from whiplashing. The waves came bigger. No lightning, no thunder, just the rain. It fell like poured gravel, and the fiberglass shook like it was coming apart. I tucked Dri's head tighter into my chest. The next wave threw us. We landed side-on into another wave. The boat whipped up the wave's face to the crest and hung there nose-down like a pendant before it dropped. We went underwater.

This crazy vision came to me down there. I was inside the mind of a fish looking up at the storm on the surface. My sky warped. My stars scattered, and my moon was ripped from its orbit. It rolled away, leaving the world with a new gravitational pull that made everything six times heavier. I didn't think we'd ever rise to the surface.

We stayed underwater for what felt like a minute but was probably a few seconds before we were ripped upward again, this time inside the wave. A moan moved into me from my feet and buzzed up my body and rang my bones. The fiberglass hull was bending, splintering. We broke through the back of the wave.

Dri coughed water. "I can't do that again," she said. I think that's what she said. The wind screamed like a Super Bowl crowd or a hundred thousand souls let loose from purgatory.

"I'm just glad you're awake," I yelled.

"I'm not! I don't want to be."

We had to do it again. A wave as tall and wide as a stadium rolled toward us. Even John was hyperventilating. We rode up the face of it so fast my organs shifted toward my spine and compressed my lungs. I couldn't breathe. The wave sucked us up to its ridge and then rolled away, right underneath us. It left us hanging in midair. What came to me then? Dri's sand castle. All you had to do was remember it. That was going to be the last image in my mind as I died, the one I would take with me into whatever came next, Dri and that kid on the shore that sunny day in front of Sully's. And then I hoped there would be nothing. If there was something, I would have to face Mr. Costello.

We fell. The boat almost rolled over as it slid down the far side of the wave. Without giving us time to catch our breath another wave scooped us up. This one had jags and peaks, a mountain range of black water. "Matt?" Dri said.

"Yeah?"

The wave smothered the boat and sucked me down into darkness and backward in time to Woodhull Road, three years earlier, the car crash under the elevated train. The windows that hadn't been shot out blew out. My eardrums felt blown in. The twisting crunch that totaled Mr. Costello's van had only lasted a second. This—being crushed inside the wave—lasted much longer, and it wasn't happening in slow motion either. I never would have been able to imagine a body could spin so quickly underwater. The boat rocked to the surface.

Dri was gone. The railing she was tied to had pulled out of its fitting.

I thought I saw her in the face of a wave. When the boat stopped spinning and hovered in the trough, and my arms stopped whipping around, I was able to put my hand to my chest to unclip my life-vest strap. John unclipped himself and lunged for my hand. "No way," he said.

"Get off me," I said. I twisted his hand away and pressed in on the buckle to click the release.

"Matt, look," he said. He was pointing backward, over his shoulder.

I turned to look and didn't see anything. When I turned back his fist smashed my face. Lights out.

# 41

## *NAVIGATOR'S LOG, AUGUST 31, 06:21 HOURS EST*

*Captain Braswell is scrambling helicopters to coordinates 40.025651 by -68.664551, where a small vessel has been sighted.*

# 42

I woke up I don't know how much later. The storm was still raging. I went to unclip my safety strap, and this time I blocked John's hand. I clicked the buckle and was free of the boat. I washed into the ocean with the next wave and swam toward where I thought I'd last seen Dri.

I found a bright orange splash on the other side of a mountain the color of sludge. Dri's life vest. She was waving her arms. I swam down the wave to her. "Look," she said. She pointed to a pink light shining off a wave. The light swung at us and blinded us. Then I heard the *chuck-chuck-chuck* of the helicopter. A yellow box hit the water and exploded into a life raft. Dri and I climbed aboard. A safety cage dropped down with a guy in black scuba gear. He took us both into the cage. The hoist jerked us up. I kept screaming for the rescuer to look down into the water. John had washed out of the boat. It had capsized. He was swimming toward us. Another mountain range of ocean was rolling at us. The water was falling apart as it rose. The crests broke off the wave and slid down its face toward John.

"Wait," I said. "He's right there."

"No time," the rescuer said.

"We can't leave him."

But we did. The copter lifted us out of the wave's path. After it rumbled under us the sea was empty. John was gone. I turned to Dri. She was gone too. The helicopter was gone. I was alone, nowhere, and now I knew I was dreaming, or dead.

# 43

## *NAVIGATOR'S LOG, AUGUST 31, 07:08 HOURS EST*

*Helicopters have been recalled. The small vessel was actually a lost cargo container and not small. It's reported to be big enough to sink a ship. It was probably tagged with GPS but our crew fired a GPS bullet into it anyway. Salvage teams have been notified and will locate and sink the container when the storm abates.*

# 44

I woke up I don't know how much later. I woke up twice actually. The first time I came to only halfway, and I didn't like what I saw, so I closed my eyes again. The monster waves were gone and so were John and Dri. The idea of being strapped to a small boat out in the Atlantic Ocean, all alone? No, I wasn't ready to believe this was my reality. So I clamped my eyes shut and forced myself to give into my exhaustion, and I guess I passed out.

The second time I opened my eyes must have been a good while later, because the seas were almost calm. The hard rain was back, though. Dri and John were back too, passed out on the floor of the boat. Dri's life vest was ripped at the shoulders, but it had stayed on her, at her waist. John wasn't wearing a vest. His was still strapped to the railing on the other side of the boat. I was trying to piece together what had happened when Dri told me. Her eyes barely opened, and she didn't lift her head from where she was, facedown on the boat's floor. "He did it," she said. "Your idiot friend. He came out with a safety line and latched on to me. We reeled ourselves in, between the crests. Why?" she said. "Why'd you do it?"

John didn't answer. He wasn't moving. My hands were too heavy to lift to my life-vest strap. I was pinned to the railing, but I could reach John's shoulder with my foot. I nudged him with my toe. He pushed my foot away and went back to sleep. His hands were a bloody mess.

Now Dri shook him. Her hands were rope-burned too. She still didn't have enough strength to sit up. "Hey, idiot?" she said. "Why didn't you leave me out there? I wish you would have just left me out there."

"You couldn't tell me that before?" John said. They both passed out.

My shoulders were cut where the life vest had burned into me as it kept me tied to the boat. I couldn't hear out of my left ear. I shrugged and figured what the heck, I might as well pass out too.

John was sitting next to me. He was shaking my shoulder. I winced and pulled my shoulder away. Dri was still passed out on the floor of the boat.

John rubbed his knuckles. "I think I broke my ring finger," he said, or that's what he seemed to say. I was reading his lips.

"What?" I said. "I can barely hear you."

"When I hit you." He showed me his finger. It was bent. "Head of rock you got there. But we knew that already. I didn't make my fist tight enough. My pinkie too."

"Good," I said. "My face feels terrific, by the way."

"Doesn't look it. You're uglier than you ever were. Have a nice black eye there in a bit. How's your neck? Whiplashed you pretty good there. I won't say sorry."

"Don't."

"You don't want me to."

"I don't."

"Let me say this much," John said.

"Don't say anything. This is crazy."

"I know."

"No, I mean this is totally wrong," I said. "Why didn't you let me go after her?"

"You'd leave me out here all by myself?"

"I was going to say the same to you, and anyway, what are we waiting for here? We're nowhere. We're nobody."

"Matt? You might want to unbuckle yourself from the railing."

"Why?"

"We're sinking. Maybe we better wake her up too."

"Now there's an idea," I said.

# 45

## *NAVIGATOR'S LOG, AUGUST 31, 10:48 HOURS EST*

*End of mission called at 10:46 hours EST. All souls presumed lost in the wake of Carlotta. RIP, Martins, Gonzaga, Costello, and Halloway. May God bless you, dear children. May God keep you safe.*

# 46

We dropped the engine, gas and all, to shed weight. It wouldn't start anyway now. The boat still took on water. Its nose was splintered, and the hull was cracked. The water seeped in slowly. We bailed with our hands, and that was all we could do. We'd lost the distiller setup, the tarp, jugs, paddles, tools, rags, everything but the bloodstained sail, which was too worn and torn to hold water. The storage cabinets had smashed open in the storm.

The sea was full of garbage. Spilled cargo, broken furniture, plastic lawn chairs, a basketball. The storm's wake dragged it along with us in clumps. The water was the color of tarnished silver. The rain was cold now, but soft. We caught it with our mouths and laughed at one another, at how ridiculous we looked, three bedraggled kids sticking our tongues out at the sky. Our wet clothes hung so loosely on us I could have sworn we'd been shrunken, and we had been, I guess. Dri went from cracking up to crying, back and forth. I man-cried, or how I thought a man should cry, which is to say I just made my face look tough and angry when all I felt like doing was bawling for my mom. John looked like he always did, no emotion, maybe half a smile here, an eye roll there when Dri's sniffling was too loud for him. We were losing it, and more than that, I was losing her.

She didn't want to be next to me anymore. I was going to ask her why, until I realized I probably didn't want to know the answer. If I so much as looked at her, she cried.

The sky had a mad, haunted glow to it, white embers. The waves were fast but small, and they didn't break. The storm had cleared out the sharks, but for how long? I didn't care if they came back now. A coil of electrified wire was shorting out in my head where John had hit me. My eye twitched.

Behind us came a creaking noise. I was afraid to turn around. I gasped inside and Dri gasped out loud when we dared to look at it: a whale, a hundred footer. Now two whales. Three. They were ganging up on us. I sat back in the sinking boat. I was done. Dri sat back too. I tried to hold her hand but she wouldn't let me. And John?

John cried.

"Get up," he said.

"Why?"

"We're saved. They're logs. They're giant logs."

"So? How's that save us?"

"Can we start with this?" John said. "They're not sinking."

• • • — — — • • •

We climbed aboard the logs with nothing more than the life vests we were wearing, the bloodstained sail, and JoJo's phone, which didn't work anymore but which I'd been keeping in my pocket. Not that I thought we'd live, but on the off chance we did I wanted JoJo's and Stef's parents to have the pictures, the same ones that were my last connection to Dri before she hated me. "You're mad because I didn't swim out after you, right?" I said.

"Matt, no, okay?" she said.

"I tried, but—"

"I know. John told me. I can't talk about it. I wouldn't even know how to. My head hurts. I can't think. I don't want to either. I don't want to think." She shimmied toward the point where the logs were highest above water. They were banded together at one end by an iron chain as thick as my leg, or as thick as my leg was before I got onto the boat two weeks earlier. The logs crossed each other at slight angles. Where they were chained, their ends overlapped like the spokes of a tepee that had fallen on its side. One of the spokes rose a few feet above the water, and we straddled it. Sitting on top of the logs we could keep ourselves mostly out of the water. The parts of our legs that stayed in there too long puckered and bled heat into the ocean. Dying of hypothermia at the end of August. None of it seemed real anymore. I started thinking I'd died in the storm, and this was some weird limbo where you didn't care what happened to you.

John patted the log. "They can't leave this stuff out here," he said.

"Why not?" I said.

"They're huge." He was right about that much. The logs were the biggest trees I'd ever seen, as wide as I was tall. They were tattooed with Japanese kanji. "You can't have something as big as a city bus drifting into the sea-lanes. A ship runs into it, you get a *Titanic* situation. We're saved, I'm telling you."

"We'll see about that," I said.

"You'll see, I know. You're going to survive this thing if it kills me. By tonight we'll be watching towboat TV."

But John was wrong.

# 47

*A few hours after sunset, day fourteen . . .*

The sky cleared and the wind came back cold. We needed to huddle to keep warm, and Dri forced herself to be wrapped in the sail and shiver with us. The dehydration cramps wouldn't stop. My fingers and toes tightened and twitched. A knife jabbed my right kidney again and again, with my heartbeat. My eyes throbbed and the stars pulsed. I thought I saw the ones JoJo had pointed out to me, Hercules or Heracles or who cared anymore.

I'd never forget the gush of blood that hit the surface when the sharks jerked him down. I knew Dri would never forget it either. John, though? I didn't think he'd sweat it much. I bet he'd forgotten about it the second we paddled far enough away so the blood slick was out of sight. "That's why they call him the Iceman," I said to myself. Or maybe I wasn't talking to myself. Maybe I wanted John to hear me. He did. He looked away. Dri turned toward me. "What are you talking about?" she said.

"How'd it feel, Johnny boy?" I said. "The crack of his skull vibrating up the hammer, up your arm, into the hole in your chest where your heart is supposed to be." This was why Dri couldn't stand me anymore. I'd let John kill JoJo.

John nodded. He almost smiled even. "I knew you figured I did it."

"You're sick, John. How were we ever friends?"

"Matt," Dri said.

"He was a day away from a bacterial infection that would have stopped his heart," I said.

"A long day away," John said.

"*Matt*, he didn't do it."

"He did. Look at him. He isn't even bothering to deny it."

"John, you really are sick," Dri said. "What's wrong with you? Why are you letting him think this way?"

"He'll think what he thinks," John said. "I don't care anymore. I don't. He wants to believe I'm a murderer? Fine. He's right too. I would have done it if I had to anyway."

"You *did* do it," I said.

"He *didn't*, Matt, for the last time."

"How can you be so sure?"

"Because *I* did it," she said. She turned to John. "Tell him, John. You saw me. I know you did. You pretended to be sleeping, but you had one eye open the whole time we were on that boat. You watched me do it. Go ahead and tell him how I did it."

"Why are you doing this?" I said to her. "Why are you lying, taking the blame for him? You're covering for him to protect me. So he and I can still be *brothers*, right? So I don't totally and completely despise him."

"John was right," Dri said. "It had to be done. I didn't think John would do it, and I still don't. I also didn't want you to think I was a murderer, in case we . . . if we ever were rescued. He—JoJo—he was talking to himself in his sleep, I thought. But after a while his eyes opened. He was talking to Stef, saying he was thinking maybe he should join her. He knelt and prayed to her, and he was crying. I sat next to him. He said he felt her calling out to him, whispering his name over and over. 'Do you think I'm crazy?' he said. 'That I hear her voice?' 'No,' I said. 'I heard her too.' I pointed to the water. 'And I see her. Look.' The sun was coming up, but the moonshine was still bright on the water. It was beautiful, a shiny line that led to the horizon, a strip of silver cutting through the cleanest gold. I said that maybe it was a message from Stef. A map, a trail that led to where she was waiting for us. 'I just want to be with her,' Jo said. 'That's all I want now, Dri. To hold her hand again. To laugh with her. Do you think I should go?' And then I—oh my God, I can't believe I did this. I want to tear my skin off and escape from *me*. I said, 'Go. Be with her.' He kissed me and thanked me and slipped into the water. I sat back and pretended to be groggy after nodding off."

"That's not the same as hitting him in the back of the head with a hammer," I said.

That made her mad. "I might as well have pushed him," she said. "I'm insane, truly. I was before I did it too. I'd have to be to think I'd be able to live with myself, to think I could be with somebody like you after doing something like that. Killing my cousin's boyfriend."

"You didn't *kill* him," I said.

"I didn't *stop* him, you jerk! He was my friend. How do you forgive somebody for that kind of treachery? That kind of betrayal. How do you forgive yourself? You just don't."

"Dri," I said.

She cut me off. All she said was "No." She shrugged my hand off her shoulder and crawled as far down the log as she could to get away from me.

"It'll be okay," John said.

"Are you out of your mind?" I said.

"She did it for you. She did it to protect you. That doesn't go away, that feeling. It never goes away. It might take some time to come back to where she lets you see it, but it'll always be there, deep in her where she'll never be able to cut it out." He studied Dri and nodded. "Tell you what. I like her now. I like her a lot. Her telling you that? That was the bravest thing I ever saw."

# 48

*Morning, day fifteen, the last day . . .*

The ticks between time stretched out again. Commercial jetliners, minor glints and distant hum, took years to cross the sky. Thousands of fins. No. Just jags in the water. Dri was as far away from me as she could get, at the last part of the log before it started to angle underwater. I let myself slip off the log. John tried to pull me back onto it. "We gotta hang in," he said.

"Really we don't," I said.

"You never know," he said.

"Sometimes you do. Yeah, let go of me. I'm done."

"Not yet you aren't."

"You look bad too."

"I feel better than I look," he said. "Now quit being a wimp and get back up here."

"Get back up there, Matt," Dri yelled. "I'm serious. I'll be madder at you than I am now."

"Why are you mad at me anyway?"

"Just get back up," she said. "Stop being an idiot."

"You heard her," John said.

"I don't know why you want to live so bad," I said to John.

"I don't know why you don't. You have that nice girl over there ready to fall in love with you all over again. Quit moping. You'll see."

"Why are you doing this?" I said. "Why do you keep trying to save me?"

"Right about now I got nothing better to do."

A gull had been circling us for hours. It was alone. It tumbled into an updraft. Its wings were wrong, flimsy like cheap cloth. It dropped down fast and perched on one of our logs. It was shaking. Its left wing hung limp.

"Leave her," I said. My throat was a gritty pipe. "We're dead anyway."

"So's the bird," John said. "It'll give us another couple of days."

"You really want another couple of days out here?" I said.

"Shh." He was arm's length from the gull. He grabbed her by her broken wing. She didn't fight him. He covered her head with his fingers and started to twist her neck.

"John," Dri said, "let it go. I'll kill you. I don't know how, but I will. You can't eat raw bird anyway."

"Sure you can."

"It's sick too. *You'll* get sick. I'll gouge out your eyes."

John let the bird go, except it didn't go anywhere. It stayed next to John and looked from John to me, to John.

I was too tired to laugh.

The bird looked up and flew off. John and Dri heard it before I did. *Chuck-chuck-chuck.*

John gripped my shoulder. I had to punch him to get his hand off me. The helicopter came close. No basket stretcher dangled down to us. No safety ropes. No Navy SEALs in high-tech wet suits. A guy in work clothes leaned out the shotgun window with an actual shotgun and fired a long-tailed streamer into one of the logs. The streamer pulsed fluorescent pink. Another guy leaned out with a bullhorn. He was laughing and waving, and John, Dri, and I looked at one another like, What do we do? John shrugged and waved back. The guy yelled down to us through the bullhorn, *"We're not here to rescue you."*

"Truly appreciate that!" I said.

*"We're spotters for the salvage crews. We're here to tag the freight. We don't have any ladders or anything to pull you up. We're short on gas and have to get back. We'll send somebody along shortly. You all right?"*

"Perfect! Never better!" Big thumbs-up.

He thumbed us back. *"Okay, help's on the way then."*

"Take your time! We'll just be right here. If we head out, it'll only be for a bit, and we'll leave a note."

"Shut up, Matt. Save your voice."

"For *what*?"

The helicopter swung away. We watched until it disappeared into the haze that blurred the horizon, and then we watched some more. We watched and watched and no one came back, not even that messed-up seagull.

The ship broke the horizon line an hour later. When it was a few minutes away, John said, "Okay, here's the story. Stef died the way she did, JoJo committed suicide with the sharks. We leave out the part about the conversation you had with him."

"No," Dri said. "No way. We play this one for real."

"Don't do it, Dri," John said. "Keep it simple. You're not going to be helping anybody here with that kind of thinking. You'll only be hurting yourself, your parents, JoJo's mom, and Matt too—Matt especially. Hey, even I'll feel bad if you do it."

"Do what? Tell the truth? At the very least, I was an accomplice. If what I did deserves punishment, then that's what I want. If the courts or whoever decide it doesn't, I'll just punish myself on my own. Sounds like a win-win for everybody. You two get another shot at life, and I get a shot to pay back the life I didn't save. Don't look at me that way, Matt."

"What way?"

"Like you still . . . Look, you guys say what you want, but I'm telling them what happened. If our stories don't match up, they'll start looking at you guys too, like what are they hiding? It's simple: Just tell them what I did, for God's sake."

# 49

I fell the first step I took on the freighter deck. It was too steady. They split us up right away and put us into cabins. I couldn't lie down without wanting to throw up, so they put me in a rocking chair, and I felt really good. They hooked me up with two IVs: one sugar, one salt. "You want to see yourself?" the medic said.

"What do you mean?" I said.

"I figure you might not want to be alone the first time you see it."

"See what?"

He brought me a mirror. I didn't recognize myself. My face was fried and my lips and tongue were swollen.

He treated me for burns on my shoulder where my life vest tore into me. I'd need an operation on my left ear. I still hear the whoosh of the ocean even now.

Later the doctor came in and asked me to stand on the scale, and I was able to for a few seconds. He measured my height. "How tall were you when you went out on the boat?"

"A little over six feet, I guess."

"Well, now you're a little under."

"How does that happen?"

"When you don't eat, your bones shrink."

"That fast?"

"Your slumping doesn't help. Be proud of yourself."

"*Proud?* I can't see her, can I, Doc, just for a minute?"

"Let her rest, son." He gave me a sleeping pill, and boy did it work fast. I fell asleep right in the rocking chair.

I woke up in my bunk, but how I got there I don't know. I got myself into the shower and lay down and fell asleep there. They woke me and helped me get dressed and wheeled me into the captain's kitchen. Dri and John were already at the table, in wheelchairs too. We all looked shell-shocked, and Dri looked away.

I went from one hundred and seventy pounds to a hundred and forty-six, and I set out to put back on every pound right then and there. They fed us Jell-O first. Then ice cream. Then I was into fried eggs, boxes of cornflakes, and frozen pizzas. The captain laughed. "Slow down," he said. "There's plenty more."

Dri gagged and hurried away to the bathroom and never came back. John didn't even look up from his plate. "Do you have any more rice pudding cups, the big ones?"

We watched a movie, John and I, I forget which one, a comedy. It was funny but we didn't laugh. I fell asleep in my rocking chair. When I woke up, John was gone. The medic said, "He told me to tell you you're boring. He's playing cards with some of the guys. You want to go down there?"

"Can I see her?" I said.

"She's sleeping." He wheeled me to my bunk, hooked up my IV, and I passed out.

When I woke, the bunk was too quiet. The wind roared inside my head. I put on the TV loud and felt better. A guy came in and said a detective by the name of Kreizler wanted to talk with me.

The detective and I sat and I rocked and told him everything, or pretty much everything. He was a nice guy. "They say the odds are eighty percent that without GPS on that boat you should have died at sea," he said. "I don't know how you lasted that long. I mean, how did you not give up?"

"I gave up," I said. "It's just dumb luck I lasted."

"João's mother would love to speak with you, Matt. She'd like to meet you when we dock in Newark."

"I can't," I said. "Not yet. I wouldn't know what to say."

Kreizler nodded. "You talk with her when you're ready." He patted my shoulder gently, more like he rested his hand there, but I winced anyway.

"Where did we wind up, by the way?" I said.

"What do you mean?"

"In the ocean. Like near England or something?"

Kreizler smiled. "They found you about eighty miles away from where you left. Who knows if you were dragged out and back in with all the crazy winds, but you didn't end up far from where you started. Life's like that, take it from me, an old guy—and it's a good thing, trust me. Hey, I'm really happy," he said.

"Yeah?"

"Driana's account, John's, yours—they all link up perfectly. Almost perfectly. You left one part out of your story."

"I did?"

"John told us. Driana did too."

"I didn't see anything. I swear. He was in the water by the time I woke up."

"Matt, nobody is going to file charges. Everybody understands."

"Can I talk with her?"

"She's gone. Her father took her home. His helicopter picked her up an hour ago."

Kreizler took JoJo's phone but said he'd send me the pictures.

# 50

They flew my dad out to the ship the next day. My mom was looking after John's mom in the hospital. She was doing okay, my dad said. He pulled us into a hug. That was the first time he'd hugged me since before Woodhull Road. He cried and we didn't. John and I didn't want to be all bunched up like that either. We were burned and my arm was in a sling. I'd dislocated my shoulder. It was on fire. I had to break out of the hug.

My father extended his hand to John. He nodded and gulped. "Thank you," he said. "Thank you for saving my son."

"We saved each other," John said.

"Thank you, John," he said. "That was a beautiful thing you did, going out there with Matt." He pulled John in for a hug, and John let himself be hugged this time, and then he hugged my dad back, pretty tight too.

• • • — — — • • •

An ambulance met us at the dock. A few photographers were there. These security guys blocked them and we ducked into the ambulance. They had my dad sit up front in the shotgun seat. He hesitated half a second before he got in. We took a slow ride from Newark into Manhattan, and then across town to the Hospital for Special Surgery, no lights, no sirens. We didn't talk.

They put us in the same room. They thought we'd like that, the nurse said. They had the rocking chairs there for us. We rocked and watched some morning talk show or other. I couldn't understand a word anybody was saying. They all talked too fast. And the makeup. Why? And why did it take two weeks lost at sea for me to notice these things?

John needed hand surgery. He'd be going home that night. My ear surgery was more complicated, and I'd be in for a few days. A nurse leaned into our room and said she'd be coming to get me in a few minutes.

"Nervous?" John said.

"No. I mean, what could happen at this point, right?"

"Well, you could always die on the table."

"Why'd you do it?" I said. "Why couldn't you let me go? To get her, I mean, during the storm. Without the rope. I wish you would have let us both go, and you stayed strapped into the boat. Then we all would have gotten what we wanted. You get to go home, Dri gets the sea, and I get to be with her. Because this? This here, right now? This is worse than dying with her. This is being dead while she's gone."

"You're welcome," John said.

"I hate you," I said.

"I know you do."

"We're even now, right? Is that what you're thinking? I took the bullet for you, so you came out onto the boat with me? Except we'll never be even. You saved me from going out into the storm, you saved her for me, in my place, and oh, by the way, I got your dad killed."

"It's just what happened."

"I'm so sick of you saying that. No, I owe you, and I'll always owe you, and I'll never be able to pay you back, and I hate you."

"Bullet or not, Mr. Carlo, my father, Dri—none of that matters. I mean, I was mad at you for maybe a day after that night, Woodhull Road. Making me keep living when my dad was dead. Giving me the chance to run. The choice. And then I was grateful to you, that at least somebody was left to see my mom through the funeral, the years after that. But I would have come out on the boat with you anyway."

"Why then? Why'd you come out there with me?"

"You were my brother." He grabbed the remote control and clicked to ESPN.

The nurse came in. “Your dad’s just down the hall in the prep room, waiting for you. Mom too.”

“Thanks,” I said. I got into the wheelchair and she wheeled me out.

“Matt?” John said.

“Uh-huh?”

“Good luck.”

“You too,” I said, and those were the last words we ever said to each other.

# 51

I can't watch movies anymore. Everything seems fake. For a while, right after we got back, it was the other way around. Everything in the here and now looked weird, too fragile, like it wasn't supposed to be there. Like if you touched it, it would crumble or end up being a sham, hollow. I don't know, everything looked like it was going to float away. Gradually, it all started coming back, the weight of things. The noises brought me back—car horns, shrieky laughter, crazy people screaming at each other over a parking spot. The crowd. I was back in the crowd, trapped.

Maybe a few days into senior year, after everybody stopped bothering me about the boat, I reached out to Dri on Facebook. They made me join first too, to leave her a message. That's how crazy I was about her, getting myself out there on social media, putting up with those sidebar ads asking me if I wanted to date seventy-year-old women in my area, because I said that my age was eighty-eight, figuring that would be enough to scare off most friend wannabes. My profile picture was a screenshot of the Francis Ford Coppola version of *Dracula*, when the count appears as his real age, which is like five hundred or something. The day after I sent Dri the message, her page went offline. I left a message on her phone and didn't hear anything, and then when I tried again, the number was dead. She was gone.

I found out she didn't take the year off after all. She went up to Harvard right away, a few days after she got back. I tracked down her mom and she told me.

Her mom really wanted to take me out to lunch, but I couldn't do it. I just wouldn't know what to say except I didn't want to talk about the boat, and all I wanted to do was be with Dri. One thing I did want to ask her was how she and Mr. Gonzaga were doing, but I didn't. I left a message for Dri with her: Could she ask Dri to call me? She said she would and Dri didn't. Her mom gave me Dri's new mobile number, but I didn't call it. She'd only cancel the number, and I didn't want her to go through the hassle. Enough was enough. She needed to forget me, and I guess she did.

On a cold, clear day in early December I found myself downtown in some Wall Street guy's conference room for my Yale interview. We were high up in an office tower. The harbor seemed small. The ocean behind it went on forever. Three of them, I faced. "So what was that like, talking to JoJo's mom?" one of them said.

JoJo. Like they knew him. Like *I* knew him. It all felt so far away, farther than it should have for a near-death experience just three months in the past. I didn't know how to answer. The whole interview was like that. I think I was blowing it on purpose. I just wasn't up for trying so hard and then getting rejected. "Weird," I said, and that's all I said.

"She wrote us a letter."

"Who?"

"Mrs. Martins. Her father went to Yale. Did you know that?"

"No."

"She said you were incredibly gracious. That you spent hours talking with her."

I nodded. "Yup."

"Uh-huh," the guy said. He looked at the other two. One of them said, "Matt, you're a hero."

"Why?"

"You don't think so?"

"I didn't save anybody out there but myself. I didn't even do that. My . . . John Costello did."

"How did it change you, son?"

"*Change* me?"

"Your time on the water."

I excused myself and left.

• • • — — — • • •

They let me know pretty much right away that I got in. I guess they needed a really crummy sailor from Queens to round out the class or something. Mom, Dad, and I went out to celebrate. This was a week before Christmas.

We went to a steak house in Manhattan. The woman at the table next to ours got fish, a whole snapper. I excused myself and went to the bathroom. I locked myself in the stall and thought I was going to pass out from the sadness. I can't eat meat anymore either, I mean hamburgers and steak and all the stuff I used to love. I know I'm supposed to eat it. I'm a carnivore, from a long line of carnivores going back five hundred million years and who knows how long before that. But since I got back from the boat, I can't eat anything with eyes, I have no idea why. Maybe I just feel bad for it, the poor sucker who got caught, I guess. Too bad I'm not a big salad guy either. I eat a lot of pizza these days, PBJ. I'm doomed, heart attack at fifty, so much to look forward to.

We ended up ditching the steak house and going to Patsy's that night, and I picked at my slice. When we got home, I tapped up my iPad to finish a paper I had due the next day, the last day of school before Christmas break. My fake-creepy-old-man Facebook account popped up with a notification in my email. I had a message in my in-box, first time ever.

Yup.

# 52

I met her two days before Christmas at a diner on the Upper East Side. I was a lot early, she was a little late. She stopped short when she saw me sitting there in the booth.

"Wow," she said.

"Uh-oh," I said.

"You look different from who I remember."

She did too. Older, sadder, impossibly beautiful. She'd changed her hair; it was simpler, pulled back. I realized I'd never seen her in anything but jeans and a bikini. She wore a dark gray skirt suit and heels, a lawyer or banker, the kind of person who ran things, not the kind who would hang out with a guy like me, jeans and sneakers. "I have to go visit one of my old teachers," she said. "Catholic school. The nuns. Gotta look like a *lady*, you know?"

"Sure. I always wear skirts when I visit my old teachers. You look smoking hot though."

"You're totally adorbs."

"How's Harvard?"

"How's Yale?"

"I guess I'll find out."

"No!"

"'Fraid so."

"Oh my God!"

"Shh."

"I'm totally psyched! I knew it!"

"I didn't."

"I *did*, for the record. I *told* you. I want that duly noted."

"It's in the books."

"I'm so happy for you! And your dad didn't even have to buy them a building."

"We just got the projected expenses work sheet. By the time we pay them, they'll be able to build one."

She swung around the table and sat next to me and hugged me and rested her head on my shoulder. It was the last thing I expected and the only thing I wanted: that it would be the way it had been. We kind of collapsed right back to that first day on the beach, when she tucked her number into my hand and I knew I was totally messed up for life, because once she got to know me, why would she be with me? Yet here she was. Here we were, holding hands under the table, drawing little circles into each other's palms. And then it all fell apart, tears from nowhere. "I see you and I can't stop remembering," she said.

"I know."

"You too?"

"No. I see you and I want to be with you, and the last thing I think about is the boat. I think about making out with you in my parents' junk-filled basement, discount DVD cases everywhere, while we're pretending to watch a movie."

"I think about you all the time. All the time. I think about them too, but you most of all. How's John?"

"I don't know."

"I thought that was going to happen. That breaks my heart, but it makes sense, or about as much sense as me dreaming about you and knowing I can't be with you."

"Why though? I don't get it."

"You do though. I didn't think we'd live, and I couldn't watch you die. If he went after John or me, you wouldn't have stood for that. He would have killed you too or maybe first."

"But if you didn't think we'd live, why'd you—"

"I couldn't see it. Couldn't see you die violently. If it was going to happen, I wanted it to be in its own time, as peaceful as it could be, or with less horror in it anyway. I thought we might go quietly, together. I know now that I never really thought I would have to live with this. I guess I'm going to have to though, huh? I guess I'm just going to have to do it, to keep on going, knowing that the nightmare might sneak up on me in the day too, in the mirror when I brush my teeth and I see Jo."

"We can help each other."

"I don't even know how to help myself. I'm a mess, and I'm not about to mess you up too."

"I'm already messed up. We can be messed up together."

"I have to figure out how to be with me before I can be with somebody else. Be with you. I can't stop thinking that he might have made it."

"No way."

"We did, just two days later."

"He wouldn't have made it through the storm."

"He stands there. He doesn't look angry. He's so lost."

"He's not. He's with Stef, the only place he ever wanted to be. The JoJo you see is the one you've created."

"And you?"

"Me?"

"How's Mr. Costello? The one *you* created."

"He's there. Not as much, but he knows where I am. He still wants to tell me something, I have no idea what. I'll never know. How are your folks?"

"Same. Working at it."

"Good."

"Is it? I don't know. I wish it would be one way or the other, clean."

"We all do."

She nodded. "Do you hate me?"

"I love you, like crazy-crazy love you."

"You're horrible. How could you say that to me? God, you're an idiot."

"I know. So, as I think about this whole conversation we're having here?"

"Yeah?" she said.

"You're saying I still have a really good chance then, right? That's what I'm getting from you anyway. Your *vibe*."

"My vibe. God, you're impossible."

"You don't have to tell me I'm wrong. You really, really don't."

She smiled. "I don't know what to do with you."

"I do. I mean, I have an idea about what you can do with me. I have several ideas."

She hugged me—hard too, and for a good while. "Maybe, Matthew," she said.

"Maybe what?"

"Maybe someday." She kissed me fast and then pulled away, and then she leaned in for a longer, harder one and lingered, and then she pushed away really hard and left without looking back.

"Someday," I said. "Okay, that's not a no anyway." I ordered a milk shake and two plates of fries and needed to ask for a second bottle of ketchup.

# 53

The day after graduation I went right back into school at the local community college. I took an intensive EMT course over the summer and now I'm working with a hospital ambulance. I'm telling myself I'm saving money for Yale, but we'll see. I ended up deferring for a year. I have until next month, Thanksgiving Eve in fact, to let them know whether or not I'll need a room in New Haven come the following fall. They check in with me once in a while. How am I feeling? Am I leaning toward coming or not? "I can't say yet," I say. I do know that I want to change my major. Instead of forestry I'm thinking I might want to go premed. Dri was right. I'm not cut out for the desert. I don't even know where the Great Basin is. I'd like to check out Rio though.

I still live at the house just uphill from Woodhull Road. All the old triggers are there. The ballpark, the elevated train, every time I see some idiot shove some poor guy around. John was right though. Those triggers will be everywhere, anywhere, any time. My solution is this: If I see wrongs I can't right I call the cops and roll on. I don't look back either. I turn the corner, onto my street, and sometimes Mr. Costello is there. I don't turn away from him. I go my way. Once in a while he follows me. He doesn't mean me any harm, and he isn't bleeding anymore. The wounds are gone. He can talk now, but he doesn't.

The nights I'm not working on the ambulance are the hardest. I dream of the sea. The Atlantic. It burns cold in me, the temperature of the water after the storm tested and tasted me and decided in the end I wasn't worth swallowing. I found out we were at the storm's edge, never near its heart, where the Coast Guard was risking lives to save ours. Still, I'll never be able to forget the thrashing. That nightmare drags me in its gritty wake and leaves me broken and thrown, pieces missing. And then I wake up, and the longer I'm on my feet and moving around the better I feel.

A few nights ago I was coming home from a double shift on the bus, which is what we call the ambulance. I stopped to fill up my brand-new very old car with cheap gas at the broken-down station a mile from the house. The station was full service only. While I waited I thumbed through the pictures Detective Kreizler Dropboxed me from JoJo's phone. I do that a lot. I was watching that video the four of us made when we were a few days out on the water, when JoJo was trying to reassure us we were going to be okay. Dri was saying, *We have each other.* I paused the video. I touched my heart to be sure the medal still hung there. The dove of peace

Dri slipped into my pocket while we were at the diner. That's when I noticed him. John. He was inside the mini-mart, at the counter. I remembered too late the station was around the corner from John's house. He used to work there. He was buying milk.

He looked exactly the same. He didn't look happy, not sad either. He didn't strike me as somebody who had a lot of worries or hopes. He seemed mildly content as he checked his phone and traded a few words with the old man ringing him up at the cash register. He paid for the milk and went.

I could have called out to him. Instead I waited for him to see me. He didn't. He headed away, up the block toward his mom's.

I hear through my mother he started at electrician school, nights. She's constantly after me to give him a call. She says we owe it to each other to reconnect. She can't understand why we wouldn't want to reach out to each other. My dad doesn't say anything about it. He puts his arm over my shoulder, the one that healed well. My hearing still isn't great on the left side. The right one works fine though, and that'll do.

I started hanging out with this girl from EMT school. I knew her from around the neighborhood, going way back. We were in a lot of the same classes at school, before I transferred to Hudson. We were pretty good friends in junior high, as much as I had friends back then. She just said it out of the blue one day: "We should go out." So we did. I liked her a lot. I felt the click, a deep affection, a bond that formed there, but after a couple of months I started to drift away. Maybe I do have love for people, but I don't know if I want to be in love more than once in a lifetime.

My bus is busy. On any given night I'll meet ten, sometimes a dozen or more new people. Patients, loved ones, the ones who love. I'm with them for half an hour or so, an endless agony for them as they deal with the surprise of what's unfolding in their minds, the realization that they're the ones this time. That they're being dealt tragedy out of the blue, that nothing will be the same. I try to make that half hour a little less rotten for them, to calm them, to touch them gently on their shoulders and tell them without words that everything will be okay when most times it can't be. Yes, I lie to them, to get them through. I speak softly and hope they'll steal some of my quiet and walk underwater with me for the space of a few breaths, and then I never see them again. But I never forget them either. Not a single one. I remember their eyes. They're all so different but so much the same. They glisten with awe. I figured it out, how to live in the city and get away at the same time. I lose myself in the crowd.

I feel Dri with me too, as I'm moving through the bustle. I hear her laugh, a little too loud, too true. I close my eyes and I see hers, the color of the ocean the day we met. The first word I whisper when I wake up every day is "Someday." And then I think, maybe someday is today.

You know, now that I think about it, the way he came out of the gas station convenience store, the way he hesitated at the door for half a second, maybe John did see me, but he just kept going.

# ACKNOWLEDGMENTS

Thank you to Anna Orchard, for saying in her lovely British accent, "I'd like you to write me a story about children lost at sea." David Levithan, for friendship and kindness that borders on ridiculous. Jodi Reamer and Alec Shane, lifeguards, for even more ridiculous generosity and for taking me in when I was a bit adrift myself! Bess Braswell, Lizette Serrano, Antonio Gonzalez, Jessica White, Rachael Hicks, Yaffa Jaskoll, Carol Ly, Megan Bender, and my dear friend (and favorite singer) Emily Heddleson. Penny Hueston and all my friends at Text, especially Michael Heyward, who is a brother to me. And my editor, teacher, and pal Nan Mercado, whose mind is as wondrous and beautiful as her heart. Risa Morimoto, I love you.

## ABOUT THE AUTHOR

Paul Griffin loves being out on the water—in a boat with a working engine. Once, when he was a kid, his uncle's leaky old boat stalled. He was adrift less than an afternoon and in the relative safety of Long Island Sound, but being stranded like that was scary enough to get him looking for higher ground. Now he lives two hundred and fifty feet above sea level in northern Manhattan, where he works as a volunteer EMT. He wrote the novels *Ten Mile River, The Orange Houses*, *Stay with Me*, and *Burning Blue*, all for young adults. Visit him at paulgriffinstories.com.